Seam Busters

STORY RIVER BOOKS

PAT CONROY, EDITOR AT LARGE

Seam Busters

A NOVELLA

Mary Hood

THE UNIVERSITY OF SOUTH CAROLINA PRESS

© 2015 Mary Hood

Published by the University of South Carolina Press
Columbia, South Carolina 29208

www.sc.edu/uscpress

Manufactured in the United States of America

24 23 22 21 20 19 18 17 16 15
10 9 8 7 6 5 4 3 2 1

Library of Congress Cataloging-in-Publication Data
can be found at http://catalog.loc.gov/.

ISBN: 978-1-61117-498-4

This book was printed on a recycled paper with
30 percent postconsumer waste content.

I

One of the new micro-mini bumblebee-size spy cameras caught Vicki Malachy pocketing—if you could call it that—a generous scrap of the new Crye multicam fabric into her bra. Juki, her mama, who was nicknamed for the bar tacker she ran on the other end of the mezzanine, didn't even get to see her go. King and JaNice simply appeared right after lunch and asked Vicki to step downstairs to Mrs. Champion's office, "Right now." This is called "being walked out." They tag team, and nobody around looks or speaks up; coworkers and friends swallow hard and just keep on pretending to be sewing. King went with Vicki, guiding her in case shock and swooning set in or she got some wild hair to flee or run amok. Or she found a way to retrieve the scrap and toss it away. It didn't matter. They have her on tape, and multicam isn't scheduled to be fielded in Afghanistan until summer 2010, so it is more or less a controlled substance, so new you can find it online as multisham looking somewhat like the real deal but without the fine-tunings or the flameproof high-tech magic features the new digital camouflage has. It can also be sold as genuine, which it isn't. Okay for hunters—deer don't use infrared detection—but bad for the troops. The fake stuff won't wash, but the dyes do, right down the drain; a few launderings and you're naked to eyes as well as infrared. It isn't about national security and troop safety only; it is also a copyright issue. All the knock-off artists need is someone using a color copier and posting it online a patch at a time. Sooner or later they'll have it mapped out and duped and our troops—and everyone else's—could be buying and fielding knockoffs on eBay from Chinese "tailors." Is that what Vicki was up to? It wouldn't have mattered if she was planning to make a G-string for herself or a blanket for Jesus in the manger. She was out of there. And even if they didn't have her on film, which they did, Frazier is an "at-will" employer. They have Vicki's signature on a document—everyone signs it to be hired—accepting that the company doesn't need a good reason, or any at all. Silent as they stepped up onto the bridge to cross the cutting floor toward the inner offices, King kept Vicki moving. Although she was usually chatting or crying about something—she was their drama queen in boy belts and hoop earrings and a pink mohawk—she was not crying or chatting now. It was shock. King kept his hand on the outside of her elbow in a very official way, as though he professionally minded if she fell down the stairs, but otherwise was personally uninvolved. No one ever remembers the walk down the stairs. There is a kind of blessed morphine the mind pours into the moment of job amputation; it generally gets you through severance and to your car, maybe as far as Halfway Home, the drive-thru package store that used to be Pure, just behind the Laundromatic. Meanwhile, JaNice pulled a plastic Food Lion grocery sack out of her back pocket, snapped it open, and began clearing anything personal from Vicki's work station, including the glamour shot of her and the snake, her donut cushion, a small magnetized flashlight, a gold lamé purse, and a sequined hoodie with half a vending machine bag of Cheetos in the kangaroo pocket. Food is absolutely forbidden on the floor; you can eat outdoors on the patio or in the break or conference room, that's it. And don't leave any food in the refrigerator in the break room over the weekend. "Attention: These permisisses spayed for bugs ever Friday," the night cleaner, Miss Cora, has posted. She's the same one who posts the "If you sprinkle when you tinkle" signs in the restrooms. There are a lot of things that aren't allowed, including sandals, to spare toes from being broken in accidents. The company doesn't allow hovering—they call it "standing on the seats"—in the bathroom stalls instead of taking the time to lay down one of those fiddly tissue covers, which are supplied and often dispense by the handful or in pieces, which may be a motivation but no excuse.

Sometimes Cora just scrawls on a scrap of tractor-feed printer paper from the recycle bin, "What the matter with you all?" Once she wrote, "God is watching." Some heathen wrote a pungent response, and the sign vanished in an hour. Also verboten: smoking anywhere indoors or within fifty yards of the entrance and wearing inappropriate and revealing attire, especially if what that attire is revealing is tattoos or piercings between navel and thigh top. Also prohibited—these are firing offenses, with no warnings; consider the handout sheet you read when hired as your one and sufficient warning—are using "fighting words" and foul language; catfighting, even in the parking lot; bitch-slapping; wig pulling, which happened once, back when "hussy" and "harlot" were still harsh talk and not just lamely funny; and clocking in more than three tardies in one pay period. They don't allow you to do your own packing either when they walk you out. Before NAFTA, before Frazier Fabrics—when this was still part of the Meadowlark Mills corporate empire and when "human resources" was just "personnel"— they had nailed down the walk-out protocols because Sue Rollins, chronically tardy, had seen it coming and had time to get revved up, got way past buzzed and into ugly mean on vodka from her Thermos, tore the audio plug from her ear, and threw her transistor radio at the supervisor who had come to can her. Sue hurled it so hard it boomeranged on its neck strap and gave Sue a shiner. She threw it so hard in fact that when it boomeranged it slung out its 9-volt battery, causing collateral damages to a coworker's eye some distance away, damages which were—after a long and convoluted forensics process—covered by workmen's comp. As it turned out, it wasn't even Sue's radio, but she took it home. That was way before King's and JaNice's time, but King and JaNice have had a lot of practice even so. They are smooth. Just seeing them walking together toward you along the aisles on the sewing floor—especially if JaNice has laid down her clipboard and has both hands free—creates anxiety and reform in the ranks. Rebels and rule benders reach into their pockets and furtively shut down their cell phones. Cell use on the floor, or in the pod toilets arrayed on the catwalk along the walls, can get you walked out too, whether talking or texting. Somebody downstairs can "read" signals, invisible waves. At least that's what got around. It's worth believing it, even if it is a rumor and started by management. Better be safe than sorry. The women who sew know that even if King and JaNice are harmless as thunder, they're hornets for the god of lightning in the house. JaNice's nickname is "No Way" because she says it, pretending she is listening but is actually thinking of how to bust chops. "Burning daylight," she'll say, right in the middle of some new hire's answer to her brisk "How's it going?" She just walks off. The phone on her hip seldom rings more than once before she claws it up and slaps it to her ear. She works while she talks. She works while she walks. She's always picking at something, a crooked cuff or unequal allowances—trying to salvage bad work. She loves the company. She's married, but he knows he's just a man. She used to sew. Seventeen years ago she walked in the front door and signed on, her first job after high school. She has worked nights and weekends and strange shifts and almost every job. She has moved up. Not far, but she will never forget how long it took; she will not backslide. She cannot afford friends. She hates wasted time and bad work. Habitual offenders make her short list, wind up on the daily report on the supervisor's desk. It's a fine line, though. She wants things perfect. She takes a lot of antacids. She wants to look good, but if she traps out too many rats, it smells bad and so does she. She is not unkind, but she is merciless. She presents a moving target. You never know where she is. She wears trendy trainers that tip her forward, halfway into a run the moment she moves. She pisses on little fires all day. Sometimes she holds the clipboard up to her face, her hand at the top, fingers gripping it white-knuckled alongside her ear as a privacy shield against lip-readers, so she can whisper about the workers with King. They pause on their rounds, stand shoulder to shoulder, facing different directions; their eyes are always roving the floor. JaNice has everybody's number from day one. This day Vicki's number was up.

2

There is never an ad in the paper for a Frazier job opening. The company lobby is open weekdays for applicants, even if they have to leave their applications on file and wait months for an interview. They are numbered on a list, like the organ-needy. There's that list, and there's also kinship, friendship, and basic word of mouth; sooner or later there is always a chair needing filling and someone to fill it. War in Afghanistan has been good for Frazier Fabrics: "Quality Product, Innovative Method, American Pride, S.E.A.M.S. since 1987."

Irene Morgan was the one hired to take Vicki's chair. The first four hours of Irene's day one were all downstairs, mostly in Conference Room #2. No one knows where Conference Room #1 is, or if there ever was one. Conference Room #2 sounds more like a kingdom, folks conferring, interpreters, international connections, big doings. Or maybe #1 got annexed into something else and the sign on this door wasn't worth replacing. Conference Room #2 has no windows, no phones, but a good strong table, always polished. One of the two fluorescent tubes flickered and buzzed, Irene remembered, the last time she worked here. Irene thought it was the same flicker now. Tradition is important to Frazier Fabrics.

Mr. Frazier's father began the tradition in the 1970s and 80s, and since they went "divisional" and his son Scott took the lead, he himself has been photographed with all the presidents since Ford; the walls are filling with handshakes. There is one strictly local photograph—a panorama—from the ceremonies at the setting of the new flagpole.

Irene moved closer to see her own face in the crowd, but she couldn't. Just her elbow, as if she had her hand up to keep the sun out of her eyes. Or were they saying the pledge? But that would be hand over heart, wouldn't it? For Irene it would. Everybody looked so young!

She stood there remembering so many things she had forgotten in the years since she left to take the job at Happy Time Clocks. Only eight dollars a workday more at first, but over seventeen years, disallowing the occasional twenty-five cents an hour raise and incentives she might have earned at Frazier as well, it had made more than a fifty-thousand-dollar difference, more than three thousand dollars a year, a little which had made a lot, had made all the difference. She had known it would; she had done the figures before she even talked to Deke about it and sold him on the long view. That was the good of his being a farmer—a man who plants crops and trees; he knew how to wait on the turning season, the accumulation and averaging of the years. She knew it was worth it. It was harder work in some ways, on her feet more, but all she had to do was stand—and stand it—for as long as she could. She knew how to stand. She knew how to stand it.

From her first paycheck she had bought some industrial-strength surgical hose and started out, as her mama would have said, the way she meant to wind up, with trim ankles and no varicose veins. Her daughter Jenny had a piano very soon that first year, paid off paycheck by paycheck, her own piano, not a rental, and lessons. Sometimes she still played for church, evening services and revivals mostly. All three of the kids had needed braces and got them, and with the Hope Scholarship, Davy had finished two years of college before he joined the army after 9/11. He'd made a career. 101st Airborne. A staff sergeant, he was "over there" now. His wife, Sherry, and their two children lived in Kentucky; their second baby was three months old. Davy would be home from Iraq for the baby's first birthday in December, if all went by plan, then back on another tour—Afghanistan in February. Jenny had gone on through college on the Hope, loved school, and was teaching eighth grade social studies in the county she grew up in, commuting to classes in Camden for her master's in summers and at night. Easy enough when you are young and able; it is only looking back that it seems impossible what you can accomplish bone tired. Jenny and Kev, her husband, were both teachers, but Kev was studying for his Ph.D.; he wanted to be a principal. Tonya, the baby of Irene and Deke's almost empty nest, didn't want anything but freckled Brad Barnes and freckled babies of her own, and he wanted her and most of the same things and still did. They were leasing to own a quarter section across the creek from Deke and Irene's hundred acres—big help for Deke since Lucky and Brenda, their longtime tenants, had retired and moved back to South Carolina. No man should have to work that hard alone, but when two who believe in it and are hoping for a profit work together turning hay or spraying fire ants and thistles or tagging cows or sweating and swearing the privet and kudzu out of the fence lines, it doesn't seem so much like stupidity or exile to be a farmer.

This time Irene wasn't applying for a sewing job at Frazier Fabrics because of the children. Irene was there for Deke. He had a cough. Some sun spots on his hands and those Popeye arms of his and places on his face needed looking at. And he was beginning to lean toward the ankle that didn't get set right two years ago. He had the VA, but there were other things besides insurance. She wanted to buy him a Gator, so he could motor around on chores instead of walking or riding the tractor. Sometimes in the evenings they would share the pedal boat on the pond, feeding the carp, listening to the martins, watching the clouds, churning themselves along on the sky reflected in the water and dreaming dreams like rank beginners. He'd farmed chicken and beef his whole civilian life, since his war ended. He was so glad to be home, under clear sky and out of the jungle, he wasn't worried about rain. Didn't need to, for years and years. Weather patterns had been changing, though. The drought years had been hard on the fields and wells; the couple had drilled deeper and been buying hay, even had to lay some out in the summer. And this day, while she was at Frazier, filling out employment information and waiting on her hiring interview, the hauler was there loading up the spring calves for sell off—all of them, not just the steers. Someone else could pay to fatten them. She and Deke didn't need more heifers. Irene didn't mind missing the roundup; she'd hated to hear the cows, though, all night long the night before bawling in the lot, with the fence and grove between them and their babies. They got as close as they could and wouldn't give up until they dried up. Every year when the truck drove out and away, the calves were bawling too. They could hear each other; they knew each other. It never helped to turn up the radio or TV; you heard them with your heart.

Irene used to help Deke with roundup, with anything at all to do with the farm. They still laugh about one early anniversary when she had some bruised ribs from a barn incident and Deke gave her a head-gate because she was not strong-armed enough to dose the cows. Cows don't run at you; they just lean, and hard enough that she was crushed against the gatepost. That was the last time he shopped for her at the feed and seed store, though.

She even took care of the broiler house at first. No more. No more starting each day easing into the crowded chicken "factory," with its autofeeder, power windows, and twenty-four-hour daylight, carrying a five-gallon bucket to gather up dead chicks, many of them pecked to death. She now has a flock; she loves her own special chickens, green-legged free rangers, bantam golden Sebrights. Irene swears that no chicken on earth is smarter: "They just have sense." They take care of the Japanese beetles, and, Irene believes, they'd run off the snakes too. She believes they know their names. They fly to her, hurtling along with bowed wings, and she feeds them shredded cheese. Deke can't see smart and dumb the same way—would they come to her if there were no cheese?—but it is okay with him if she keeps them for their company even if they are ugly, which they aren't. They are beautiful. They all have beautiful names, except the one with the funny comb like Frankenstein's bride. Still, she's "Bridie."

Whatever delights Irene delights Deke. He nailed up a peach crate to the front porch wall for the one hen, Mercy, who likes to sleep high but close. Way high, so nothing can jump up to her. Each evening Irene sets up a little pole ladder Deke invented, notched to lean against the crate, and Mercy hops right up it, rung by rung, and settles down. If

Irene forgets to set it up for her, Mercy paces back and forth on the porch railing, waiting, antsy, murmuring, readying like a basketball player about to make a free throw. One night when Irene forgot the ladder, they found Mercy on the ceiling fan blade bunched down next to the motor housing. So that's something else to remember: porch light and fan *off*. Sometimes another of the hens will come and share the same dorm, but usually it's just Mercy, alone. Irene's like a kid at Easter gathering the tan eggs. Most of the time the chickens lay their eggs in their nests in the car house, but once in a while Mercy will deliver one on the porch, right on the welcome mat. When Deke finds a bronze feather with its black lace, he'll pick it up for Irene's collection. She has a vaseful. When her hens die, she takes it hard, buries them with honors and prays them back to God. Deke loves that about her, but in so many ways she remains a mystery. They still study each other, still matter. That well has not dried up.

Irene has always canned and frozen and put up from the garden and orchard and berry thickets, and she used to sew for the girls and now makes clothes for the grandies, and she has always kept a good house, with a fresh pitcher of sweet Luzianne waiting for Deke in the refrigerator summer or winter. Pretty old-fashioned life, with a lot of laughs, even if buzzards are always circling somewhere, high in the sky, waiting. That's just life on the land. Marketing the animals makes her sad, but she's no vegetarian. "Just don't name the pig," her granddaddy used to say. That's pretty much her policy on it too.

Irene's search for a "town job" in the late 1980s wasn't a comment on Deke's providings, Reaganomics, or farm life in general. Deke and she weren't conspicuous consumers. They always had enough cash for new and nice things for Sunday and school, and plenty to share any day or hour. They had the old cluck-cluck tractor that Deke restored—and which he still trusts like a friend even though he's got a Kubota now too and a decent truck with a ball hitch—and bicycles for the kids. After the kids were all settled in school, though, she began thinking about wage pay and insurance. All the wives were doing the same thing, or selling Tupperware or Avon. She first worked at the Frazier plant sewing, and then when she heard that Happy Time had dental benefits, she went there. After Irene got the job at Happy Time in Camden, she and Deke bought a secondhand car for her to get back and forth. After a few years, when Davy got his license, she found three other women on the same shift and pooled. It had all worked out just right. Carpooling freed up the wheels for Davy to drive to school. That got him, and his sisters too, off the bus. Things like that made a difference at their age. She knew that from her own country childhood and town schooling.

When Happy Time closed and was outsourced to Mexico, all that changed, almost overnight. Irene and the other shift workers showed up one Monday and the Happy Time gate was chained. No management showed up. There was yellow caution tape along the fence, and a notice was posted, all the notice they got. Time, someone said—the only laugh of the day—had run out. Even the machines had been crated and carted south. Her whole rainbow, steady-even-floating life popped like a bubble and headed for the drain; there hadn't been a whisper or rumor about it. Now a lot of places had closed or were bottom-lining, offering part-time work so they didn't have to bankroll benefits. Irene had been looking for months, since before Thanksgiving. Her unemployment and COBRA benefits were about up. Irene had said she'd never show her face back at Frazier or in any other sewing plant, but she had changed her mind. She had thought she was well done with sewing, with being dragged forward all day with the cloth as it went under the needle, doing her part but never finishing anything, just shoving her piece on and picking up the next one. Now she was thanking God for the second chance.

This time she had hardly read the paperwork Frazier's human resources had handed out, the hefty spiral-bound of rules, addresses, weather info for snow or flood times, whom they are to notify if Irene can't or won't, whom she is to notify if and when and before, just scanning the pages to find where to put her signature. She was that sure, that ready: this was it because what else was there? She'd looked. She turned back to the stack of papers before her, trying to pay attention, choosing options. There weren't so many options: beneficiaries, numbers, avowals, permission to be "surveilled," next-of-kin disclaimers. One page she had set aside, one question to come back to.

Irene looked to see if Mrs. Champion was still out of the room. She even looked around the ceiling and scrutinized the Rocky Mountains in the framed lithograph on the west wall, in case she was being "surveilled." She had already noticed the missing corner—clean cut—of the ceiling tile in the ladies' bathroom. She had restrained herself from saluting, or mooning, it. She went back through the papers now, pretending to read others again, and finally worked her way through the stack to the question she had skipped. She faced it. Had she been a member of the union? Were they allowed to ask this? For three months, when she worked at Kroger almost thirty years ago, she had been. Not even Deke knew that. She was a teenager. She wasn't married then. Considering how things went, and what she had been through then and since, she couldn't see that there was much to confess or brag about. She never attended a meeting. The only impact she could see it had made was that the steward—he was the chief butcher—had learned her name and phone number. He was the only one. He did not call on union business. She accepted nothing from him. He got nothing out of her except dues. Irene smiled. That was the last job she had before she met Deke and married. She filled in the box beside NO.

Mrs. Champion now returned with a photocopy. She didn't hand it to Irene. She clipped it atop the tax information on the inside cover of the folder. "I just wanted to double-check on something," she explained. She laid her palm on the file and studied Irene. "You've been through all this before; we keep the files forever. We're glad to have you back, but unfortunately it has been too many years; you don't qualify for the 'rehire' prerequisites, so you lose all former seniority dates and benefits. You have to start over just like you have never worked here." Irene knew that. "You have to start —" Mrs. Champion hesitated. "You have to start at almost the same place you started before, $1.05 more than minimum wage." She glanced up, in case Irene had any ideas or regrets. "But minimum's more than it used to be. Everything has risen. You knew that, about the grace period for coming back, at the time of your leaving. You signed forms. I have the forms."

Irene nodded. She had no ideas or regrets. "I signed all the new forms," she said, pushing the stack back. It would be ninety days before insurance would kick in. There were other little details, and the possibility of incentive pay as well as an annual raise, depending on her production performance. Irene jotted these things into her notebook also. Mrs. Champion checked each sheet in her custody before laying it in the file, checked again, front and back. "You're in good shape," she said, and started toward the inner office. It was almost lunchtime. "You will meet with Mr. Al Grayson, your supervisor, at 1:30. After lunch. He shuts his door; nobody knocks during his quiet time. You'll see what I mean. He's on the mezzanine. You know where the midline companionway is, by the old cutting room? Things have gotten moved around. They've even installed three little scary pod bathrooms along the walls on the mezz level. They're not Port-o-lets, and they are permanent, and they are modern; there's just something about that fiberglass skylight. Also, they sort of—well, they're not really, but they seem—" Mrs. Champion whispered, "they seem springy. Spacey. Who wants to be hunkering down way off up there in the air?" She cleared her throat. "Most of our ladies still come down to ground level."

Irene didn't say anything. She was trained; she thought of it as "factory-broken." She knew all about squatting on schedule, and like most factory workers, especially those on production lines or working for incentive, she preferred not to need a break and drank water sparingly and only for health. It wasn't the stairs; it was the time it took. After you got good at the job, after you made production, there was the hope of incentive to keep you in your chair. You got to know exactly how many seconds a long seam takes, a turn, dropping and picking up something, stopping to answer a question. Time was ticking all the time somewhere in your mind, like a taxi meter, running while standing. Any interruption in the flow, in the progress, in the pace had visceral impact and consequences. "You even sew in your sleep"; that's what Deke had said, anyway. But that was before; that was her first sewing job. But then, when doesn't every stitch, every second, count?

"Mr. Grayson," Mrs. Champion was saying, closing the file. "He's in the office cluster at mid-mezzanine, and you can ask anyone where."

"I'll be fine," Irene said. "Thank you."

When Mrs. Champion had gone, Irene chose a packet of cheese sandwich crackers from the basket on the conference table. She picked up a bottle of water. She had brought a sandwich bag with apple slices in it and a shake of cinnamon. She needed caffeine, and she had decided to splurge fifty cents for coffee. She wouldn't do it every day. But this wasn't every day. She was the last one to be processed through. She was in now. She had the job! She had joined the team.

The hirees had all reported for class at nine. They had watched the film on troops in the field. It was called "Fielding the Team." They were part of the war now, part of the team. After ninety days she would get a Team Frazier lapel pin. Frazier's "product, method, and pride" were making a difference. After the film, they were allowed in the hall of the executive wing to look at the items in the glass case and photos on the wall so they could see what they would be making. When they returned to the conference room, they met the safety instructor. There was a slide show. There were some laughs and many serious warnings. It was a mixed bag. Report every scratch or accident, but don't have any. They knew now not to mess with a lockout tag or an abusive boyfriend. They knew whom to tell if they suspected someone else had problems. Or if a stalker followed them into the parking lot. They learned not to let anyone else in on their card swipe, called "crowding the door." They learned the importance of clocking out on time, within the seven minutes of grace. Failure to do so messed up accounting, who assumed you were sneaking little bites of overtime, and it could hold up your paycheck. It was called "being whistle bit."

They were given their temporary door and ID/time cards, which would be replaced by permanent cards after probation. They must report any lost cards immediately and would be charged fifty dollars for each replacement during probation, that amount deducted from the paycheck of the careless employee. They must work overtime when asked; they must work overtime in increments of half hours and hours exactly, to aid accounting. There were other rules about overtime, but they were told there would be no overtime while on probation, so please not to ask. They were instructed about other "resources." This meant mental health. Irene had put the brochure in her pile of papers to take home and—please, God—never need again. "They're there for you, but let's not tie up the hotline," the safety leader said. "Everybody's sad now and then, but I'm not talking about something chocolate and MIDOL can cure, arright? But if you are feeling dangerous, let somebody know." They knew now to give all wheeled vehicles, even laundry carts and the postal clerk, right of way. They knew to wash their hands before sewing. They knew not to wear lotion on their hands or arms as they sewed the new camo—this was not protocol, just common sense—in case lotion messed up its ability to deflect infrared detection. They knew not to discuss anything about what they were sewing even with family and certainly not strangers. Irene's son was in the field. She wondered what he would make of the new camo. She wondered what *she* would.

Irene's head was brimming with all sorts of first-day information. A bell rang. Someone walked by, headed for the time clock, then others, then the rush began toward the break room and the downstairs lavatories. Someone was microwaving popcorn. Another was heating up something Italian. The break room and the conference room shared a wall. The relaxing workers sounded like hens. Irene pocketed her change purse and went along. She watched the little bracket-mounted TV offering satellite news of the world while she waited in line. That TV was new, she found out, bought with proceeds from the vending machines, along with a machine that grinds beans and makes fresh-brewed coffee each time you put in the coins. Irene hated the smell of burnt coffee. This was a real treat. She decided to go off the rails of her budget and put in an extra dime and get cappuccino. She carried her cup back to the conference room. She hoped this would not be a preview of her lunchtime every day; the break room was chaos. She shook out another cracker sandwich. Someone going past recognized Irene, faced about, put her head around the door, and then came on in. It was Aldine. "I can't believe it," the woman told Irene. "Look at us!" They hugged. When Irene stood up, Aldine hugged her again. "Girl!" they said simultaneously, patting each other's hands, palm to palm, double high fives, like it was good, all good.

"I'm back." Irene figured that pretty much said it all.

"I thought you were smarter than this!" They had been classmates at school, and for a time while their babies were little, they had attended the same church. Aldine and her family had moved away. Aldine worked in the front office in administrative support. She was a blond now, and she had a Wolff tan. No wedding ring, but a turquoise on her thumb. "Ad sup—that's a typist who knows Word and PowerPoint," she told Irene. "That safety thing y'all sat through a while ago? That was mine." They did some catching up, just like anytime they met. But it had been years. Frazier—and Happy Time—had a way of soaking you up and wringing you out, so there wasn't anything left to spread around. Irene didn't ask about the wedding ring, but Aldine had always been able to read her mind.

"Two years ago," she said, "we found out he likes 'em taller and younger. Where you gonna sit?" Aldine asked her.

"I don't know."

"Don't let 'em put you in that back corner. No way to jump if there's a fire. I'm assuming you're on the mezzanine?"

Irene shrugged. "I report to Mr. uh—" she checked her notes— "Grayson after lunch."

"Mezzanine it is," Aldine said. "You're in the army now. I've heard that's some really voodoo fabric, but you'll get along with Grayson. He's fair." Aldine walked around the conference room. "I can't believe they painted in here again. Remember how they paint? They believe in white paint. And buy it in sixty-gallon drums!"

"Maybe this is some of the same paint from when I was here before," Irene said. "Maybe they won't change colors until they use it all up."

"And then they get halfway around, run out, and have to order another sixty gallons!" The blocks looked velvety and smooth with the latex layers. Aldine was studying new posters, a series of inspirations around the whited walls. She hadn't been in the conference room since last fall, during the annual open insurance options campaign and lecture. Mrs. Champion came back through, trailing popcorn fumes and chatting on her cell. She gave them a look. Aldine was okay; this was her lunch too. She didn't even turn but just waved. Irene was already feeling that nervousness, though, that tension in the stomach, about—about everything: trespasses and debts; territory; loose lips; tale bearers; great, maybe impossible, expectations; humiliations. It is one thing to get a job, another to keep it.

"Ray Silverstein," Aldine read, looking at the poster's tag line. "Does he work around here?"

Mrs. Champion looked troubled, sensitive about the—as she thought of it—Jewish issue. In her tenure they had had Muslim Arabs, a Christian Arab married to a Greek, some Buddhists not always Asian, proud gays with T-shirts to prove it, and they had two workers in wheelchairs and one work-pusher in a leg brace and boot. They had a materials handler with palsy. They had Jacky, who was just Jacky. They had Hispanics. Right now they had three Hmong, a Thai, a Korean, all sewing, and a Chechen data entry clerk. The Kenyan IT tech had written home for his brothers to come on over. He was sending them money. There was a former nun. There was a Philippine newlywed married to a Cuban boxer with a fixer-upper condo and no credit. There was a street preacher, Sister JereAnne. They had a tall, lean, very stylish black Muslim academically suspended all-American college basketball star vegetarian in cotton-and-rubber shoes who had really brought down the mood at last year's Memorial Day lunch hour barbecue cookout but then won friends and the limbo contest. There were Hindu Mauritanian sisters in saris and with bindis. There was a Pakistani intern in audit. The company nurse, Mrs. Giddings, was an Adventist. But Frazier Fabrics did not have a single Jew working there, as far as Mrs. Champion knew. How would you ask? How would you recruit? How would you know? Names didn't always reveal. For a moment all three women looked at Ray Silverstein's poster with "Compensation satisfies; it does not motivate." "No," Mrs. Champion—sighing for deeply felt and unspoken reasons—said, "he doesn't work here."

For very different reasons, Aldine—who thought from her own work experience the poster's verbs were exactly backward—said, "I didn't think so."

3

"What did you do, when you were here before?" Mr. Grayson asked Irene. He was not the first black man she had worked for. She did think he might be the first black man who floor-bossed for Frazier in this plant, and certainly the largest person in the plant. A big man. She was old enough to be his mother. "Wise Ol' Al," his nameplate—held by an owl in a graduation cap and gown—announced. He was an Alabama fan. He'd been a fullback, had photos and honors all around. Framed clippings and headlines, a jersey, crimson and white everywhere, Roll Tide! pennants and banners, pompom fringe hanging out of the closed file drawer, souvenirs and desk toys on sills and every other flat surface. A game ball on the file cabinet. Bear Bryant motivational quips tacked to the corkboard, taped to the door and its window. Had to be honoring the legend; he was too young to have played for Bryant. Last year's Boss's Day mug with a little football-shaped balloon on a stick and containing some untouched sugarless candies. A thriving philodendron snaking its way around the wall, strapped to the ceiling tile frames. In the center of the chaos on his desk was a clearing about the size of a place mat, with a Bible and a can of Diet Coke, both open. The bench by the door was covered with printouts and notebooks and procedures and inventory reports, and there was a folding chair popped open in the space left. He did not ask her to sit, so Irene stood.

"I wasn't fired," Irene told him. "I left to—"

"Pursue other interests. Yeah, I know," Mr. Grayson said. He had already cleared that up with Mrs. Champion. "But while you were here, what did you do?"

Irene replied, "I cross-trained. Bar tack, pocket rivets, zippers. Gents."

"Gents," Mr. Grayson said, tickled, tasting the word. "What else?"

Irene's shoulders and blood pressure rose a little as she thought of the machines. How, day by day, week by week, the fearful and challenging machines had become real, had become partners with her hands on them, so that what had been a strange and nightmarish dreamscape became as familiar as her own kitchen, but the size of two football fields. "Belt loop cutter, pocket welter, pocket hemmer, yoke machine, auto sleeve, Adler bar tacker not Juki." She knew they had a Juki now. "Label sew, zippers, brass and nylon, like I said, gents. Serger, of course. Horizontal finisher, inseamer, seamer." She hesitated. She hated to add the vapor press; it was her worst job, a nightmare in summer with the steam, and frightening. Nobody wanted that job; it was no place for a beginner. She had seen, everyone had seen, what it did to Carly. Of course, it did something *for* Carly too once she signed papers not to sue when the unmaintained steam line broke. After the third set of grafts on her face and arms, and rehab, she came back to work wearing an eye patch and a turban, then later a wig, with a job pushing the mail cart. She had that job for life, it was said. Mr. Grayson was looking at his papers. He glanced up, waiting. She sighed. She was replacing someone who had sewed; maybe the vapor press with its hateful movable bucks wouldn't be an issue. "Seam buster."

"Seam buster?"

"Yessir." She was already thinking how to tell it so Deke would laugh. How Mr. Grayson was an Alabama fan but when he scowled he looked like a bulldog.

"You bowl?" He leaned back in his chair. It creaked. "Bowling team is the Seambusters."

"Men's," she remembered.

"Gents," he said. He loved the word like a new toy; he was going to play. "No. Not anymore. They lost interest. I mean, how many men work here anyway? The ones who do—" He shrugged. "We're not bowlers. So the ladies—you know y'all were Pins and Needles? Yeah, well, the ladies hated it, so they just took over the Seambusters name and the shirts." Irene felt apprehensive, years of factory experience, nothing to do with him at all, anxious about lingering too long or wasting time. Maybe Mr. Grayson had never worked production. It was too soon for her to ask about incentive. If she had been invited to sit, she would have gotten up now.

"I don't bowl," Irene said. Maybe she could. She didn't have babies at home. But she was away from Deke all day; why would she want to be away at night? And a ball and shoes would cost something, plus league dues. She and Deke had bowled together a few times, early in their marriage. She had even sipped a little of his beer, pretended to get happy, but she already was. Another time they had played putt-putt at a state park, when they were camping with the kids.

Mr. Grayson brought his chair back level. Irene blinked. "I've got news for you," he said. He held his hands up, showed her his palms, a train-stopping whoa. "You can't iron this new camo. All sorts of things it'll do for you if you keep in mind not to wash it in phosphate detergent or starch it or iron it. I'm sure they told you downstairs some laundry product does what they call 'enhances the IR signature,' makes it 'inappropriately bright' in night vision goggles. You could get somebody tagged. And even though it's fire retardant, you can't lay an iron on it. In brief, no steam, no vapor, no seam busting on this gig. We're on a new page here." They smiled at each other. It *was* good news.

Betty, the senior on the line, was lurking outside the door, waiting her turn; she was to show Irene around, set her up to be trained. She peeked in, pretended to knock, needing to task on. Irene noticed her flowered cobbler's apron, frizz-permed "Frivolous Fawn" hair, brave claret lipstick matching a professional manicure. Wedding band on her right hand. Widow? She looked older than she probably was. Irene glanced away.

"Is she hired?"

"She's hired, Miss Betty, we're just figuring out for what."

"Don't you Miss Betty me. I may be senior on your line but I ain't a senior citizen! Not yet." Irene could tell this was how they got along, not a quarrel. It was like flirting, sort of. Personable, not sexual. She was a Georgia fan, wearing a Go Dawgs! shirt under her apron. It wasn't Friday, but she had on the red T, black slacks, the bulldog earrings. Nobody in her family had gone to college, but they all went to the home games.

The phone on Mr. Grayson's desk rang, and he ignored it, then hit hold without lifting the receiver. It rang on. He jerked the receiver up and then dropped it like a bomb back on the cradle. That stopped the ringing. His laugh started low in his chest, a rich baritone. He pointed a finger gun at it. They had a new phone system and he was still on the rising side of the learning curve. It appeared he thought discipline, as for a puppy, would help.

"It's respect, Miss Betty," he said. "I 'preciate how long you been young." The phone rang again. "See ya?" he said, waving them out.

"Let me walk her around and through," Betty suggested. As soon as they were outside Grayson's door, Betty told her, "I wasn't here then, but I'll take their word for it: they tell me you can sew. Is there anything you *want* to do, besides go home?" Her reading glasses made her eyes large and soft, but they had a glint.

"Inseams?" Irene answered.

"I'll keep that in mind," Betty said. Meaning, think of something else; inseams are covered.

"You tell me," Irene suggested.

Betty gave her shoulder a little slap of approval and set off down the aisle. They were headed for the empty chair mid-row, just past the cross-aisle break. "You'll train with Coquita on armor carriers."

"Oh," Irene said. It hadn't occurred to her how everything had to have camo, not just the soldiers. She thought an armor carrier was a wheeled weapon.

"We'll whip you into shape in no time," Betty said. "Haven't lost one yet." Then frowned. "Well, except for Vicki. You're getting her chair. But I think she was lost when she got here, if you don't mind me saying. Her mama and I are best friends." She bent to pick up a lost label, pocketing it. "Sometimes all you can do is cry." She finger-flossed a piece of lint from the feed dog and pocketed it. All day long she pocketed things that weren't where they should be, cleaning up messes. Cheering her crew on, never grinding. She was no grinder. She had sewed. She still did. "God knows, she's been there for me." She presented Irene to the women on either side of her and down the row, no formal introductions. "Y'all, this is Irene. This is a good place to work, good people," Betty said. "Say yes." They all hollered YES. So far Irene didn't know which one was Coquita. There were women on each side of her chair. Heads had lifted all down the row and looked Irene's way, and now they ducked back to work. "This is my wild corner," Betty said. "Thank God for penicillin."

As Irene was sitting down, rolling up to her station, Betty leaned over to pick something else off the floor. "Is this a gum wrapper?" she asked. Rules about that too. She took her time, standing up again, feeling barehanded to see if Vicki—why not? who else?—had stuck Juicy Fruit gum underneath, as though the crime and the clues were all going to be local to this gone worker's stand. Irene noticed the dog tags. Betty was wearing dog tags. "My boy is over there now," Irene remembered. She didn't know if she spoke it aloud. She had tried to make it a habit as often as she thought of Davy, to remind God.

Betty used her toe, made sure the floor plug was in straight, then powered up, flicked on the light, tucked in her dog tags, and handed Irene a grabbed-up bouquet of pieces of interesting fabric. "My boy's home now," was all she said. "Coquita? Show Irene how it's done. Maybe 'bout an hour? then let her go. Y'all play nice. Don't scare her off. We want her back here tomorrow."

That's when Irene found out that Coquita was the light brown jumpy one on her right with Marlboro breath and a shaved head, in a black T-shirt and camo fatigues, who asked, "Your son's in A-stan?"

Surprised, Irene had to think. Should she tell this strange-looking young woman? Not because he was married, but because he was—Davy. He was hers. Also she felt shy because of that "A-stan." Also Irene pronounced it eye-RACK not eee-ROCK. She didn't know how Coquita would pronounce it. And she didn't feel she had the right to call it A-stan. She saved that new word up, though, to tell Deke. "But he's coming home for Christmas," she told Coquita, "and then they're deploying for Afghanistan in February."

"Trained troops," Coquita said, "right here," offering her hard little hand. That hard little hand trembled, seemed to actually vibrate. Coquita pulled it back. "Yeah, I know," was all she said. "Two tours Iraq, one in A-stan," Coquita added. She called it eye-RACK also. "Iraq and Irene, Iraq and I ruin," she said, tapping her own chest, and then laughed so hard she snorted. When she sat up again, she was wiping her eyes.

The platinum blond angel-haired woman on Irene's left was Kit. She made a woohoo gesture with both hands and said, "Can you say PTSD? And all this is what they're fighting for. Plus peeing on schedule and hiking to the boonies to smoke."

"I'm glad I didn't know," Coquita said. She straightened herself up, and then she and Irene got right to work. Coquita believed in hands-on, so they used Irene's machine. Started absolutely from the basics, going down the checklist Betty left, beginning with names of parts, then threading.

"Threading's the beast," Coquita told her. But Irene's steady hands remembered how; she didn't need glasses and she didn't use a threader: she shot it over and under and around and on first try straight through the eye, goosed it a little, gave it the chachacha, looped the threads up, and clipped them. "Damn," Coquita said. "I may be calling on you—"

23

About twenty minutes later, the first seam Irene sewed through the tough light fabric was true and straight, but she had one piece inside out. She couldn't tell right from wrong.

"That," Kit commented, sewing straight-backed with her chin jutting forward, zooming along, "is the story of my life.

In your first ninety days, you can't be absent or tardy, not once, not even a minute or less late or early. No "time clock irregularities or infractions. One hour docked for any minute thereof. Habitual offenses, summary dismissal." That sort of talk amused Irene a little because she was not someone who was ever tardy; she had worked most of her adult life and did not need to learn good work habits now. But even though she was sure she had planned right and she was tired enough to sleep, she lay in bed that night imagining how terrible it would be to be late. She had set her alarm for 5:00 A.M. but then got up and reset it to 4:30. It was only five miles to the plant, in downtown Ready. She had her clothes laid out. She was ready for Ready. She couldn't do a thing, though, about her jittery nerves. Thank God the cows had mostly quit bawling, and so she lay there, beside Deke, and rested, but she didn't sleep deep enough to dream.

On her day two, Irene was in the Frazier parking lot half an hour early. She could hear roosters crowing, like old men calling *Where's ya wrist watch?* over in the old mill town. Robins singing in the mulberry thicket, and somewhere high, too dark yet to see them, a pair of kildeer. A very fresh sweet April day, with a rind of the Easter moon. Irene had her choice of parking spots. She chose one with an empty space beside her and began to read her "Daily Bread" by dome light. She kept an eye on the clock, and on her rearview. Then it was time to go on in; others were moving toward the building, no stream yet, but handfuls. Irene clicked off the dome light and started gathering things, but before she could get her door open, here came Kit in her little acid green convertible, plunging improperly and boldly down the one-way, shortcutting in from the other lane, facing the wrong way, aimed for the gate. They were drivers' sides door to door, window to window, but Kit never looked around. Irene waited until Kit got out and remote-locked over her shoulder, running like she was late. She was thumbing speed dial as she ran.

By the time Irene had locked her purse in the trunk and got to the door, Kit had ducked in on somebody else's swipe, dashed to the vending area, and was out back sitting on the picnic table with her feet on the bench drinking Mountain Dew. Breakfast. "I don't want him, I've thrown him o-u-t, and I don't care where he lands," she was saying into her phone. "He's a liar. So let him lie. He can lie and maybe on the side of the road or in a gully somewhere 'til the buzzards take him down to the ribs for all I care." She listened and then laughed, "That's it, that's it, start with his lyin' eyes." She brought her feet up onto the table, swung around, and lay flat down, sobbing up at the sky, tears in her ears. Workers looked but went on by; this was Kit. This was private. This was how it was.

The line at the clock stretched back into the building. They weren't allowed to stand in the doorway or queue up outside. Every worker had to swipe in and then stand in line inside the building, being surveilled, waiting for the clock. Someone official checked both records for that, especially in the first ninety days. All of the new hires had been warned. If anyone forgot the rules, there were notices all around, reminding. And, of course, they had signed a paper during orientation, which was on file.

By the time Irene got in line, nineteen back from the clock, she had heard all about what would be listed in Thursday's *Messenger* as "a domestic altercation on Camden Street." Kit's private life was very often public. She came in now, right at the last moment, when the first person had swiped her card and headed upstairs. Kit looked stormy. Grief was under control. Her angel curls were still drying but already crisping with product and indignation. "I hate starting over," she said, but she already had—she always had. She didn't flatten her affect once she came in, figuring right that they'd all heard about it or would. She had no face to save. The one she wore was game. Kit did not even ask first as a courtesy but simply broke in line with just her left arm, leaning way in behind Jacky, the materials pusher, balancing with her right fingers resting on his shoulder. Jacky was listed as white, but he looked a little exotic. There was mystery about him. Kit, pale as a Kewpie, winked at Miss Anita, the steady black deaconess and drummer at Mt. Moriah and their front-line senior, who prophesied, "There be another one, Baby. Save the salta ya tears." Kit swiped her card through and ran for the ladies' room, leaving aromas of strawberry and ginger body wash in her wake.

One time Kit had been called out for a dress code infraction; she had showed up in a pair of inspirational short shorts pulled on over sweats. Across the butt of the shorts it said TRY HARDER. She had honestly thought wearing them over the sweats would be okay. She knew not to wear them without the sweats. Besides, it was winter. They had sent her home. "Why?" Kit had wanted to know. "Do I get to come back?"

"To change clothes," King and JaNice had told her, "And yes."

"In that case," Kit had replied. Then she had leaned on King for balance and peeled the shorts off.

"No way," JaNice had said, which Kit had taken as encouragement, not shock and awe. Then Kit had shaken the shorts out, turned them so King and JaNice could read them, had given them bullfighter's pass, said "What it says," and gone back to work.

Irene's locker was in the top row next to Sua Nag Vang's. It said so, in interesting handwriting, on the door. Irene's label holder was still empty, from Vicki's deletion. While Sua Nag opened her locker and hung her jacket, set her lunch on the shelf, draped her ID holder around her neck, tied on her apron, gripped her refilled water bottle under her elbow, and locked up, Irene waited. "You first next time," Sua Nag said. She didn't look at Irene. At first Irene did not know the tiny woman was speaking to her. She didn't know eye contact is bad manners among Hmong. Here came Kit, who opened a stuffed locker on the bottom tier, kicked things back in, peeled out of her overshirt, slammed and locked, and loped off to work. Her hair was banana-clipped up now.

Now Irene could see the ladybug tattoos behind Kit's ears and the Miss Kitty with a red bow tattooed on the nape of her neck.

"Targets," Sua Nag said, not looking.

Day two went fast. They all did. By the time Irene got her first paycheck, she had earned her second paycheck. It began to get easier. Two months to go on probation. She met with Mr. Grayson, for about a minute. All the new hires in miniconferences presented themselves for his remarks, hearing whether or not they were "where they should be at this point." They had been summoned all at once and were beckoned into the office and out quickly, one after another, like chickadees at a feeder. Irene was "where she should be" after the first thirty days and celebrated her first paid holiday, Memorial Day. Then after the second thirty days, she was where she should be, so she sewed on; she was still on track, so she sewed on and on.

4

Frazier prepared for the Fourth of July. There was bunting swagged between great bows of yellow ribbon on the old bell tower. That was Jacky's job. There were red, white, and blue twirly whirligigs along the drive, flags in the whited planters of red and purple petunias by the main gate. Unofficially, Jacky's pickup with a removable billboard in the bed—an election-year sideline he had thought up on his own— readable from both sides of Main Street, rolled slowly through town with PA speakers on the roof playing "God Bless America." He signed up for every parade but thought up something special for the national birthday every year. This year's display was pretty much the cherry on the sundae. He was going to make the national news.

Jacky was the one someone pointed out when someone else had complained at lunch that "no men work at Frazier." There was a pause as they considered him—wiry, broad-backed, shy, helpful, un-grumbling, good as gold, intense, literal, and with a steel plate in his head from something he did not remember and no one knew. He'd been dropped off and abandoned. Some said gypsies left him at the service station when they couldn't sell him. Others said he followed the goat man into town. It was said that Jacky had been neutered and that "*they* had never descended." Not word one of any of that was the truth; none knew what the truth was. He was fostered, a ward of the state, and he had thrived. He was a man now, and some of them knew it for a fact. In case the new hires didn't know, they heard all that at lunch.

28

The one who had complained added, "I meant doing what *we* do."

"No man could."

"Ya think? Or are we just pure damn idiots?" That should have been Coquita's line, but she had sprinted out back, to smoke.

"I'm not pure," Kit said, peeling her yogurt foil open, giving it a wide cat lick and then some kitten ones.

Here came Jacky. He had postcard-sized U.S. flags on little poles duct-taped to the sides of his Braves cap. When they hushed as he walked by, he stopped, as though they were waiting for whatever he had not thought until that moment to say. He was wearing his Team Frazier American Pride pin on his work vest, over his heart.

"You prouda me thih time," he said. "I ma' big prans. I hadda grill holes in my cruck." When they weren't kindled by that, he added, "I had hep sperring the wurgs." Last fall he had misspelled a crucial word on his billboards—the candidate's name during the whistlestop: FRAZIER WELCOMES BARTACK OBAMA. After that he had promised the company never to use the Frazier name without asking and to be sure he had permission to "endorse." He thought endorse meant writing, as on a check. Since then he had signed his signs "Jacky." That was OK? That was OK. He had also promised to seek proofreading help. Someone at the *Messenger* was suggested, but who would ask a newspaper person to help when it was a secret? People who worked there were bound to tell. One of the guys up front downstairs had asked him, "What if it isn't Obama?"—meaning losing or winning the election. Jacky had replied, "Whatever"—meaning Jacky would have made a billboard for anyone who came through, win, lose, or draw. That was hospitality. That was American pride. Nobody knew how he had ever gotten a driver's license, but he kept it renewed, and he had never, so far as anyone knew, gone past the speed or the city limits. Most of the time he rode his bike. Sometimes he pushed it, when he had time to stop and talk along the way.

Irene knew him. He was not much older than she was. She remembered how he had been teased in school. She started to get up and walk away.

Kit was the one who got up. Dusted crumbs. Smoothed her shirt front and eyed herself over her shoulder and shook like a lady duck. "I hate linen," she stated. "Don't wear linen to work." Who but Kit would? She tumbled things around in her purse, spritzed her throat with cologne, rubbed it on her hands, and applied the extra to her hair, then smoothed, smoothed, and clenched the curls. Next she crowned herself with her sunglasses. She was ready. She was "just running out for a minute." She had a phone call to make, but one more bit of table business before she went. "Is it a secret, Jacky?" she asked.

"Yuh."

"A good one?"

"Yuh!" He nodded his head, smiling at the floor. "American pride," he said. He grinned.

"He grins!" Kit said. She scanned the table and pointed her middle and index fingers at her eyes and then at Irene's eyes. "Don't y'all tease him, now. If it's a secret, it's his secret. Wait for the surprise." Irene realized that Kit was warning her off. Irene smiled. She made the same fingers-to-eyes sign right back at her. They all watched Kit's long legs in those low-cut skinny jeans step her way out of there, weaving through the disarrayed chairs. "You're thrilling us, Jacky," Kit called back, looking at him, only at him. Then she put her shades over her eyes and carded out at the door to the executive parking lot to make her call. It was the nearest exit, that was the only reason, but if someone offered her a ride, she'd go. They wouldn't see her till the next day. She'd take off. She took offers. She took risks. She took French leave. She took everything but abuse, and she gave as good as she got, but she kept coming up empty. And she kept coming back to sew.

Kit was the one who finally phoned "the seam buster mystery number." Irene thought she remembered the U.S. Patent number on the seam buster to be 391 3428, how it looked like a phone number, and asked in a lunch lull one day in month two if anybody had ever dialed it. She was just kidding, didn't imagine anyone had or would care—or dare— to find out. Kit dared. "Maybe he's my last and only." On a potty break, she detoured past the machine, which was still in place but shrouded.

She used her key-ring laser light, crawled up under the canvas, found the number, and wrote it down on her wrist with a fabric marker. Irene had almost remembered it correctly: 3248 not 3428. Kit was on fire to try it. Why had no one thought of this before? Why had no one tried? "That's the trouble with being married," she told them. "Y'all just give up."

Kit was never going to give up, couldn't wait until the end of the shift. They formed a circle around her on the lawn under the pecan tree as she keyed the area codes 706, 770, 404, 678 before the numbers. She'd disconnect with a scowl or a shiver or a gagging gesture at her mouth, something wrong or "off" with each one—nope, nope, nope, and nope. She took it hard. She was impulsive about random acts, had seen this as a beacon sign of kindness from God, and yet nobody worth falling for. Skunked. Every time it was a home number, not some panting billionaire who answered his own phone. "Maybe it's his limo line," she said. The last one left her furious. "I woke that one up! Who else but losers are home in bed this time of day?" She scrubbed her wrist with hand sanitizer.

"Wait, wait! What about South Carolina? What about South Georgia?" Betty just egged her right on. "How about China? How about Mexico?" No one took it seriously but Kit.

"Hell, Miss Betty, I have to be back on Monday!" Most of the time she was.

Currently they could see Kit pacing back and forth, now in the sun, now in the dapples under the executive dogwoods, making a lazy spiral; she spoke to somebody smoking, looked back at him, waved, laughed, walked on, still talking, walking all the way out to the road. FedEx and a sedan drove in and FedEx drove out, but nobody offered rides. At the table they kept checking the lunchroom clock, anxious, looking sharp to let her back in; everybody had to clock in after lunch. It wasn't forbidden to exit to the front lot, but their cards worked only one way on that door: out. Kit hadn't asked them to. She just assumed someone would let her back in—whatever, whoever. Things usually worked out. Kit generally landed on her feet, and until she did, she was flying.

31

Jacky was still standing there at the end of the table. They'd forgotten about him.

"Yuh can tease me," he said. But nobody did.

He was loved. He was a fixture. He was somehow grandfathered in. He was a sight. He was forgotten. He surprised them; he was keeping an eye out too. He was the one who jogged over to let Kit back in.

When Jacky finally sprang his Fourth of July surprise, it was a doozy. This was his finest year so far. In giant semipro house-painted letters his truck-bed billboard announced:

MOST FAVORED NATION

NAFTA & TALIBAN

CANT BEAT US

He had stapled up flags all around the sign and screwed flags to his side-view mirror brackets.

Since July Fourth fell on a Saturday, there was no official responder at the plant, but word got around, and one of the news vans drove over from Camden. Small-town story with local interest, but others picked it up. Then some CNN copyreader with an eye for punctuation jumped on it, did some research, and tied the typo to the history of the town, which had started out as Pines's Creek, because the creek rose and ran through Caleb Pines's back pasture. Early maps had it right. Later maps called it Pine's Creek. When the roads got paved and plank-bridged and Pines's Ferry closed and side-road signs went up, it was Pines Creek, because the times and the signs had changed, had caught up with the 1891 geographical protocols: no more apostrophes. The village itself had been known as Pines's—just Pines's—or sometimes in court records Pines's Post Office, which was a pigeon-holed rough-sawn pine cabinet in Pines's general store. When the railroad came in 1892 and the government named the mail drop Pine Creek, Old Caleb Pines took his name back. This wasn't about Georgia pines. This was a family name. This was family pride. He rode to Atlanta and back on the train, gone over a week trying to get it right. He was gone politicking again during the legislative session, and while he was away, folks voted to rename the mail drop. They were sick of the whole controversy and were ready, willing, and able to move on. They did. Mr. Pines didn't think they were able, and kept rounding up signatures and X's of those who owed him money or favors and swore they weren't willing, but the ones who were ready never backed down. They petitioned the secretary of state, and the election records and ballots were sorted through and certified; they won. Maybe they weren't all willing and maybe they weren't ever all going to be able, but by God, they were good and ready. That's what they named the town: Ready.

Cute little story, pure Americana. And then Jacky's truck with the billboard, taken as it was intended. Not an apostrophe issue at all. CNN aired it every hour. Jacky's truck was beamed down from the satellites, and sweet little Ready, Georgia—which hadn't been as ready in the twentieth century for the interstate as it had been in the nineteenth for the train and had gotten passed by: the interstate highway roared on by nine miles away without an exit—ready or not, on July 4, 2009, went international. The twenty-first century finally arrived, not by road at all but from a satellite. There it was. Jacky's surprise! His fresh-scrubbed '69 pickup truck, parked right there in front of the plant, beside the Georgia granite flame-carved monolith reading

FRAZIER FABRICS
Quality Product
Innovative Method
American Pride
S.E.A.M.S. since 1987

Jacky's MOST FAVORED NATION sign in the back of the truck provided angle-parked counterpoint. It was readable from both sides of Main and the railroad line as well.

On Sunday morning, it finally hit Mr. Frazier's fan. He saw it on CNN as he waited in Reagan Airport—he and his family had been to Arlington for a ceremony and the concert on the Mall. The decree went out, and Jacky's truck was towed.

Monday morning could not come soon enough. No one in Mr. Scott Frazier's boardroom—or Gibbs' drugstore or Blaine's barbershop or Jenny and Tom Croft's Hole in One (or Two) Donut Shop, or Mimi's beauty parlor, all with their signs and possessive apostrophes in place—believed Jacky had thought it up completely on his own or, as they put it, "executed" it himself. Jacky admitted that was so, admitted he had help, but his help had made him swear secrecy. Jacky was good at secrets. He knew he was in trouble, but he did not know why. This was a room he had never been in; he was abashed by its sprays of orchids, its fern-filled fireplace with a mantel clock under a glass dome, its rolling ladder along its wall of leather-backed ledgers from almost a century of incorporation, its massed and traditional splendor including a silver coffee service in use right then. Rather than stare rudely, he examined his feet and the carpet beneath them. It surprised him by looking a bit old, a bit faded. Maybe somebody had given it to them, someone they did not want to disappoint. Jacky pulled his mind back to his own troubles. He listened and listened. When he answered, he was brief and—what else?—himself. If he could do better, he would. He did not understand what they meant by "contractions," which he knew only as a birthing term, and he did not comprehend "too political" and just listened, waiting, planning to ask for and hoping to get "another chance."

He was sent back through an adjoining and less intimately grand boardroom and past the assistant's desk, to wait out in the hall. While he was waiting there, Police Chief Lazarus, "strictly as a friend," as he told Jacky, sat beside him on the bench and praised the lettering on the sign and asked him who had given him such good help, but Jacky would not divulge. He himself had done the painting; that was all he would say to the policeman. He had done most of the stencil-cutting also with his neon green utility knife his sweetheart SarahAnn Hurd, Pastor Ben Hurd's daughter, had given him for Christmas.

SarahAnn had palsy but got around great on a pair of canes. And she could swim like a seal. Jacky loved to swim, but he was a kicker and a splasher. SarahAnn was sleek and splashless. The water on her eyelashes, when she blinked open at him after diving in, tore him out of his frame. She had no idea. That was the best of all, after some of the bold women he had dated. Most of them didn't like wearing a bathing suit, or at least didn't like getting it wet. And they never did more than walk around up to their chins; they cared too much for their hair. Jacky and SarahAnn were making slow plans. Their hearts might both be heading for a wreck they couldn't walk away from, but what lovers don't risk that? Pastor Hurd, who had begun to think there might not be any grandchildren in his future, had given his consent for courtship at least and at last to begin. There was an age difference, but not much of one. SarahAnn, who was Pastor Hurd's only arrow in his quiver, had a biological clock ticking loud. But at least it was ticking. Hurd had brought Jacky along through several studies, gathered him into the flock at revival, and baptized him a year ago; Pastor Hurd had himself brought "the new man" up out of the water, well pleased. He had no pastoral or paternal doubts. SarahAnn was no spring chicken, but she was unseasoned, and Jacky was—his pastor knew from frank discussions—well-seasoned, a little salty. "Nuh mo," Jacky swore. SarahAnn was the only one he wanted, now, no matter what the Ready women tried on him.

"Fine," Pastor Hurd said. Only one warning, "Ask," he told him. "If you're sure—"

"I sure," Jacky stated.

"Well, man, when you think you're both ready and before she's an old woman, ask." They shook on it. "Ask," he said again, because he had already talked to his daughter and knew her heart, and because of the way Jacky overlooked the obvious and tended to pass the exits because he missed the signs. Pastor Hurd thought he had handled things well, until he realized he too had overlooked the obvious, when Jacky, at the end of his and SarahAnn's fifth date, stopped at the payphone at BP and called to ask Pastor Hurd if he could kiss her. "I askin'," Jacky said.

The police chief tried several approaches in Frazier's main hall, but Jacky always saw him coming. Chief Lazarus went on in to speak with the others. He told them what he thought. Jacky could not lie and was capable of only literal truth, not half-truths. He told them what he suspected. He told them what they already knew: Jacky didn't even have a clue what NAFTA was. And he sure didn't know a damn thing about apostrophes; the one missing from *cant* was missing in action, not an intentional act. This was Mr. Frazier's opinion also. "He's an idiot, not an idiot savant." Jacky wasn't an idiot, though. Mrs. Champion risked saying so. No matter; that did not rule out sabotage by someone using Jacky as a blunt instrument. That notion caused deep sighs and soul-searching bewilderment. Jacky had kept asking if the sign was spelled wrong or just not true. How could Jacky get a thing from "Not exactly"? He didn't know where to start working on fixing it, which end of the snake to pick up. He had gotten agitated, and that's when they had sent him out in the hall to chill. By the time Lazarus had gotten there, he was calm again.

"We have Department of Defense contracts," they had explained when they called him back in. Which meant what it said, to Jacky, who did not have subtextual skills. He heard it with pride. American pride. They kept saying the sign was embarrassing, and too political, and without that apostrophe almost seditious, none of which concepts Jacky could get a handle on. When Mrs. Champion explained that sedition meant treason, Jacky staggered back, almost knocking over the little table with the ginger jar lamp on it. He landed on his butt, pulled his legs under him, spring-flexed up from the floor as if he had been flung, and resumed his spot on the old rug. He wouldn't look up, just muttered, horrified, seeing all of his dreams going down the drain, "Nuh, nuh." He couldn't think of anything else to say. Exasperated, Mr. Frazier offered to fire him, but Jacky did not know it was a kind of barter. When Jacky heard, "That's all then," he just began packing up his heart and thoughts to go.

"I unna arre't?"

Chief Lazarus looked at Mr. Frazier. Both shrugged. "No," Mr. Frazier answered. "You're not under arrest."

"I fee to go?"

"Just go." Mr. Frazier had swiveled to look out the window until Jacky was out of there. No one else looked at him either. He was cut.

Cut to the quick. Only four others were in the room, but they felt like a complete jury.

Convicted, Jacky put his hat back on, the one with the American flags, and walked to the door. Then he turned back and took it off again, and there where he was standing with his hand on the doorknob, in a manly and courteous way—he did not beg—Jacky asked for another chance. Mr. Frazier thought he meant as a materials pusher and said, in his own good time, without looking around, "Dammit, yes!" But that was not what Jacky meant.

He took three tries—he was monitored on security screens—to hang his ID and key card on the coatrack in the lobby and leave. It took him three tries to solve it because he had to figure out how to swipe himself out, turn, dash for the bentwood hook, hang the lanyard, and run out the door before it could click locked again. He finally took off a shoe, blocked the door open, hung the key card, shoved out, grabbed the shoe, and then put it back on once he was on the steps. Mrs. Champion ran after him. He was busy tying laces. He had to retie the other shoe because it felt loose now. Then he had to retie the first one because it was too tight. Jacky liked things forgettably even.

"Where will you go?"

"Use yuh name?" She thought he meant as a reference, and she thought he meant *her* name, and agreed. Who would hire him?

She prayed, "Thy will be done." She meant Father God, not Scott Frazier, not Jacky Lamar Jones. She cried for a little, shook the tears off her hands, then went back inside. "Jacky has left the building," she announced. The keycard and ID wouldn't be noticed for a couple of days; on Wednesday Birdie from Cora's night cleaning crew would turn them in to lost and found.

The meeting had adjourned, and life at Frazier went on without him.

As soon as Jacky got his truck back from impound in the open lot behind the firehouse, he spray-painted the offending sign blank with primer, feeling nauseated with shame and fumes. His friend who had been helping with the signs—it was Vicki Malachy, who could not be

37

said to be impartial—wanted to put something different on Jacky's second-chance billboard: she suggested a double row of stitches all around the sign and something special in the upper corners instead of flags, since the Fourth of July was over. She suggested—in fact sketched on—little footed crosses, painted in tight zigzags so they too looked stitched, sort of buttonhole stitched. Jacky couldn't see it. "Look," Vicki said, "do 'em in black. Bold. Maybe inside a red circle." She looked around for a plate to trace and picked up the lid for the paint. Too large, but she could always redraw them. "Make an impact," she had urged him. "They're bitchin'." But Jacky was in conflict; he didn't want to say so—so he didn't say so—but he thought they looked like swastikas. In fact, they were. Nobody liked swastikas; why would you put anything on the sign that you already knew nobody liked? Golly dog! He didn't want to go through that again. Ever. He held his ground. It might have come to ugly words, though not from his mouth, but Vicki got a phone call. She took a hike way out in the yard to answer it; reception was better near the streetlight. It was Juki, Vicki's mom. The streetlight was buzzing and there were bugs. She kept slapping them away.

"Girl," Juki told her, "Where are you?" Juki was babysitting Vicki's colicky baby, Randal. Not for the first time but maybe for the last. Three hours ago Vicki had dropped him off and supposedly gone to get diapers and some Gatorade.

"My car was making that sound," she said. She made the sound. "I ran by Jacky's to see if he could—"

"Vicki Marie Westmore Malachy," Juki said. "You lyin' layabout Jezebel from Hell, if you ain't back here in fifteen minutes God bless America if I'm not—and I am!—calling Lazarus *at home* and reporting an abandoned child, plus I am telling him I think you're not just a petty criminal, you're uh- uh- a meth whore and dealin' dope and nookie on the side!"

The baby wasn't Jacky's son, but he could have been. And she'd have claimed he was if Malachy hadn't married her. They hadn't lasted six months. He was clean gone, good and gone. Somebody said the

Philippines. Somebody else said Alaska. Vicki might be pregnant again, but nobody knew that, not even Vicki; she had gone to get diapers and a pregnancy test, no Gatorade. She was sick to death of diapers. They didn't grow on trees. Life was so not fair. Vicki hadn't even bought the test; she had boosted it. Seemed to be reading the label, then picked up another box to read and seemed to be deciding something, then set the one back on the shelf and the other one dropped right into her big old gold lamé purse. It was beginning to show signs of wear, little bald spots in its glory.

"By the time they get all my lies sorted from yours," Juki was raving over the baby's wailing and writhing in her arms, "and test the Tic Tacs spilled on the floorboard—they're bound to find somethin' to keep ya for if it's only expired car insurance—you'll be in jail long enough they'll jerk you back to Jesus, if anybody can. I know this—I am done trying." She began to sob.

"Doesn't sound like it," Vicki said coolly. But she lost steam after that, finished her cigarette, threw the lipsticked filter out onto the dark pavement beyond the streetlight. It bounced three times, chipping little final sparks off, then went spent. She had come by hoping to borrow money from Jacky. And get him into bed so she could blame him, if the test turned out positive. He just wasn't listening to her very well. She gave him a hard look, but he was working on his project, didn't even notice. Vicki got in her car, tore off, didn't wave good-bye. Typical. Jacky was glad she was gone. She made him nervous. He could not trust her, because she had said—last time—she wasn't coming back. She wanted something that time too, and he had promised God and Pastor Hurd he wasn't giving her any. Now she had left, driven off mean-like, without saying a thing, so maybe she meant it.

Jacky steamed on with his sign. The Fourth of July was over, but he—and Frazier—had American pride every day of the year, and it was his project; he got to say and this time he would. He said it with gold stars. He even stenciled some on the truck's doors and tailgate. The flags on the mirrors waved on. They were nylon. Rain didn't hurt them. He worked on the new sign the whole week after July Fourth. He decided it looked fairly clear, no major wobbles or drips. He rolled it out into daylight from under the tarp-covered shed on Friday and made his round-trip run along Main before parking it at the street curb at Hardee's. There was one traffic light in Ready, and that was the strategic spot. Jacky then walked home sipping on a peach shake.

Frazier Fabrics got a few local calls almost at once. Mr. Frazier took a break and drove by the sign. This time he took it well. Dan Archer from the *Messenger* was already there taking photos. Archer got in the car with Scott Frazier and suggested they use the drive-thru for coffee. They then parked in the lot and sat talking while sipping. Archer finally asked, and not unreasonably, "Scotty, is this the hill you want to die on?" For the mile back to the mill, Mr. Frazier gave that some thought. After he walked back into the plant, he asked Mrs. Deems from HR to gather his captains. They took the sign the way he did and adopted Jacky's sentiments as the motto for their newsletter masthead, ending early a competition among employees for a prize for best company slogan. Since the story on the first billboard had aired, Frazier had been getting a lot of calls; it seemed that the publicity had not damaged the company's corporate image. Nor had Frazier's government contracts been damaged or rescinded.

Jacky didn't know anything about any furor, any calls, or what the captains were thinking now. He didn't have a phone or a TV. He was a radio man, AM not FM. He was hiding out, ashamed. Pastor Hurd had phoned Mrs. Champion to inform her that Jacky hadn't been at church and to ask if he'd been at work. So Mrs. Champion drove out to Pines Creek Park to his little aqua and silver trailer with the used tires on its metal roof to prevent rumble. The steps looked dry-rotted and iffy; one was missing. The railings looked—she could think of no other explanation—wolf-chewed. She glanced around. No chains or pen. Even so, she stood warily in a patch of clover and leaned even more warily, finally ducking her head and shoulders under the rail on his mossy porch and knocking on the bottom of his door, all she could reach. She talked up to him through a crack in the jalousies and then finally talked him out onto the porch. "Oh, Jacky," she kept saying. She had his lost-and-found keycard and ID, which she handed up to him. "People oughta talk to one another. People ought to stay in touch."

Jacky just listened. He heard amazing things. He had his job, they liked his truck, they missed him, all was good again. He knelt on one knee, meeting her at eye level. "Fuh real?" he kept asking. He had always been clean-shaved, something eternally boyish about him. Now he looked clean but grizzled, attenuated, wintry. "Poorly," as her home folks would've put it. When she explained that the others were expecting him back at Frazier, she suggested he might need to go in and get himself together. He didn't. He came right on out.

"Ready." Beaming. She walked to her car, to move things from the front seat for him, but he wanted to follow her back on his bicycle. "Lady furt," he insisted, and gestured toward the road. She drove on. He got to feeling better and better along the way. In fact, he passed her, the flags on his hat fluttering full flat open just before they turned in through the Frazier gate.

That afternoon Jacky was awarded the twenty-five-dollar WalMart gift card that had been offered as the slogan prize for the newsletter, *Focus on Frazier*. The contest had been running for three weeks, and there had been no suggestions except "Sew straight or sew long," offered anonymously. There might have been more, but the suggestion basket was supervised by a spy cam, and since the Vicki incident, those cameras were keeping it real. Jacky's winning motto was

FRAZIER FABRICS

"Seams like old times."

When Mrs. Champion had come to see him the Monday after he left his truck at Hardee's, her visit had landed on him like a rainbow, along with the pot o' gold. He thought he had been rehired until he got the next paycheck, which had credited him vacation pay for the days he had been absent. He went down to payroll and inquired. He didn't want something that wasn't his. He was bringing it back. The clerk made some calls. "You earned it," she told him. "It's paid. Vacation. It's all yours." She explained, tapping on the computer screen. She placed the pay envelope against it, to help him follow the line all the way across. She printed it out and showed him, "Paid vacation."

"They did that fuh me? Fuh me?" he kept asking. Jacky went out to the hall. He squatted, resting his hand over his eyes, his back against the wall. Donny Kilgore came along on afternoon circuit and dust-mopped around him and went on. Someone walking to and then back from the ladies' room to her desk in payroll eyed him, then described him to the clerk as "visibly asleep or sick or praying," all of which were strongly advised against in the employee public conduct protocols, especially when visible from the main doors in what was called "the executive wing" but was really the central tower. The clerk came out, phone in hand, poised for 911.

"You OK?" She shook his shoulder when he didn't respond.

"Juh thinkin'," he told her, rousing after a moment.

"No law against that," she told him.

He looked up but didn't see her walk away. He was more and more aware, though, of everything else around him, behind him, beyond him down the dim hall leading toward the modern lobby under the old iron bell high on its yoke under the peeled cedar loft: the buff-waxed terrazzo with its squeaky sheen; the green sofas and chairs gathered on the edges of the green rug with all the black and white and tan circles; the huge low silver and glass table with its industry publications and its driftwood decoration; the familiar whitewashed brick walls of the old tower; the dainty ficus and the thick bold rubber trees and palms in the brilliant afternoon light; the staghorn ferns on their bark shields; the zebra finches branch-hopping and buzzing in their huge glass cage; the sound of the wall fountain of slate and copper with its shawl of creeping fig; the languorous turn of the three-blade fan like an airplane prop; the fly settling onto one of the slats in the blinds on the middle window; the directory on its stand casting shadows across the lobby floor; the soft and hard of things and the high and low; yellow butterflies in the mounded "Miss Huff" lantana beyond the window; the breakable things and the things that would never break; the shelter of the whole Frazier plant around and over him. He felt himself in the very

42

heart of it. It was so large and strong and real and fine, he would never sufficiently fathom or deserve or honor it. This was America to him. He had never been on vacation before. He was glad to be back. Wait until he told SarahAnn! He got up and went along to work. He wouldn't replace the flags until football season, on his cap or on his truck. And he was already beginning to plan for next year. He could feel the stir, the slow turn, of deep thoughts.

5

Irene's day ninety fell on a payday. JaNice brought the checks around. She dealt Irene's toward her, and for an instant the paper in the envelope was a bridge connecting them, one moment of startling, serious linking. Their eyes met. "Congratulations, Irene." JaNice handed her a little plastic bag with a Frazier pin in it. "You've earned it." She lingered, as though she was listening to something far off. Irene wanted to take the pin home and show Deke; she didn't want to put it on right then, but when JaNice stayed, she wondered if that was what she should do.

JaNice cleared her throat. "You left in—" she began to say. The phone rang, and JaNice answered it. She turned her back, spoke fast, listened fast, then said, "No way. There were twenty-seven this morning, I counted. How many are back there now?" She paused. "Tell King. No, just tell King." Disconnected, JaNice turned back.

Meanwhile, Irene had felt herself tumbling through space. *What* had she left? What had she left *in*? She was not a rebellious breaker or bender of rules. All her infractions, and there had not been many, and none lately, were accidental or ignorant, not defiant, not willfully negligent. She didn't think she had made mistakes sewing. She was upset enough to crumple her paycheck and put it in her apron and then not be able to remember what she had done with it, then find it, keeping it gripped in her pocketed fist. Fear rose up like flame around her. The fear was not lack of courage; it was dread of courage, dread of what it could cost her, that one of these days she would decide none of this stress was worth it and all of it was optional, what Deke kept telling

44

her, and she'd "lose her grip" and lose everything. It wasn't fear of letting go of something bad; it was fear of losing something good she somehow "needed" the bad to get. Not get. Earn.

Irene came from long lines of "earners." Foothills and easier plowing had brought her people down from the mountains. The rich bottomlands had been claimed long before. What was left—thin soil on foothills smallholdings—had kept everyone digging for their lives, cropping corn and beans, garden truck and cut flowers, especially lilies, earning their daily bread. Sometimes that soil washed away, into the creeks and rivers and to the sea. That same erosion washed some of her family downstream into the mills at the shoals. She came from the ones who didn't wash away easily, no matter what. She came from people who in varying degrees believed and practiced how love suffers long and is kind. All her life, from baby bunting on, she had heard blood kin singing like they believed it, believed in the daily setbacks of time on earth as merciful lessons and blessings to understand later. She believed what her grandma had said, pointing to the admonition on the wall at the little cold-water Blue Ridge church—a church that believed in signs—where great-uncle Seaborn, one of the lily farmers, was being buried from, a church they had traveled back in time to find on its ungraded two-track lane, a church with a door for men and a door for women, with spittoons and a hand-scrawled warning: DO NOT SPIT ON THE FLOOR. The sentence PRAYER CHANGES THINGS was what had caught her great-grandmother's eye. Her granny—who ought to know—had pinched, hard, and hissed from behind her paper fan on its stick, "No it don't, Irene. God changes thangs; prayer changes we uns."

Irene came from folks who kept their spoons clean and took what was dished, the sort who tied knots in the ends of their ropes and hung on. Irene pulled herself up, squared up her shoulders. Ready. She was the sort who held out.

"You left in 1990," JaNice said. Not an accusation but a question, or a statement she could refute, if need be.

"Yes," Irene said. "Summer."

"I know exactly when," JaNice told her, with a flash of her eyes. "I got your chair." She inspected the left front side of the plate carrier Irene had just sewed. She was studying perfect seams. JaNice wasn't calibrated for finding "perfect"; she was company-trained for what was wrong. JaNice clipped a thread for Irene and laid it back down.

"Things got better right about then," Irene said, smiling. Relieved. That was blessing enough.

"If you'd just held out," JaNice replied.

Irene groped for something else to say. Her fingertips touched the envelope her check was in. What did JaNice know? What did she need to hear? Irene searched her heart. If there wasn't anything JaNice needed to hear, Irene wasn't obliged, by God, to say word one. Best not.

JaNice lingered. Irene thought of how what seemed to her to be most of her life had happened when she left that chair, and what JaNice thought *her* life was had happened after Irene left and JaNice sat down in it. As though it was the chair that made life happen! There was always going to be another chair. It's not the chair you need to hold on to. But then she thought about how she had had to get down on her hands and knees at Rock City to cross over the little swinging bridge. It was no holiday. How hard it was to let go, one hand at a time, and the other one holding on for all she was able, just to make herself crawl forward, to hold her mind to what was ahead and not look down. Just wanting it to hold still but the others walking along so easily, just laughing and talking to beat the band, making the whole span of rope and planks sway and rock.

Irene was about to say, "Funny how different it can look depending," but before she could, their little moment was over. All she got to say was, "Funny—" The phone was ringing, the Klaxon was sounding downstairs in receiving, JaNice was muttering "No way," and then she was gone.

6

Six pounds of plums or figs will make four or five pints of jelly or jam. That amount was about all Irene cared to fool with at a time, but for a few August weeks she was busy, nightly, measuring sugar, cooking up plums, and dealing with the figs Deke had gathered that day. She'd work after supper right up to bedtime, and sometimes they'd hear the lids popping as they cooled and sealed on the kitchen table after she and Deke were in bed. First thing in the morning, while the coffee dripped, she'd set the little jars away in the cupboard. Sometimes she took the time to make biscuits, and they sat breakfasting together on the porch in their twin rockers, before Deke headed one way and Irene another. Deke would even do tricks, he said, for her fig preserves. "Keep 'em coming." She was gratefully proud of the jam, but especially the batch made from this year's late plums, which glowed in the jars like she'd caught the sunlight with the flavor. She knew the jam tasted good, but she also believed it was good for them. She made sure there were jars for all their children. She was already beginning to gather ideas and items for Davy's Christmas box. She wished she could mail him jam— or sunshine—in a jar, overseas, but she never did. Besides, he had plenty of sun. She'd already sent Sherry, Davy's wife, some of this year's jam, as well as—she couldn't help it, they were so beautiful—fresh plums, a perfect boxful, by overnight. Maybe it was true, like Deke said, that there were actually stores at Fort Campbell and maybe plums in Kentucky too.

"There are now," Irene said.

All winter, on dark mornings, they could spoon that sunlight out. She knew what it was like to be a soldier's wife. Irene's folks had died young. Deke's parents had stood in the gap for her, and sometimes it was their care packages—each with a magazine or three yards of fabric or a pretty kitchen towel or a bag of candy or a packet of seeds or a card with a few perfect crisp bills in it—that got her through more than the winter's dark.

She had put up some of the plum jelly in embossed half-pints with fancy floral seals and white rings. Pocket-size jewels. She liked to take them to work and leave them on the sewing tables of the women who'd stepped away for a moment. She never could catch Sua Nag away. Finally one day she pocketed a jar and headed downstairs to lunch.

Sua Nag Vang did not sit with a group. She usually ate alone, her back to the TV, spooning up lean soup with bits of interesting-looking vegetables. She ate from a plastic bowl with a seal-tight lid, and she brought her own spoon. Her refilled water bottle, its label peeled off, stood by her right hand. Between sips, she screwed the lid back on. When she finished, she placed her spoon and the bowl and bottle in her lunch bag and left them for a minute, went to the ladies' room, then came back, gathered her things, and headed upstairs to sew again, usually the first one at the clock. She was always trying to find more minutes to work, not to rest. She always had a little smile, and her eyes, very bright, were focused on something only she could see. Irene had noticed how she didn't yack at lunch, how she seemed to be listening to something far off. How she never seemed to look at anyone. How she seemed to move in a bubble, silent, through all the racket and chaos—not lost or adrift or isolated, but peaceful.

Irene thought Sua Nag was maybe Thai. She couldn't tell how old she was. Maybe in her forties, about the same as Irene, or maybe in her fifties, maybe even nineties. She was timeless, if not ageless. Irene had seen a cooking program on Thai spices, knew that red pepper was one of the main condiments, and lemon grass. Irene did not know what lemon grass was, but the idea of it pleased her, that somewhere in this world grass that tasted like lemon grew. What would that do to the cows and their milk? She wanted to ask Sua Nag about it. Maybe she had some, grew it in her own garden and could give Irene a "start."

Irene had a gnarled old lemon verbena that had been her great-grandmother's. It had summered on the porch in a lard bucket, then been hauled back down the steps into the root cellar, where it wintered, slowly losing leaf on fragrant leaf, a few holding on until spring's last frost. Her granny used to put a crushed leaf in a glass before she poured in iced tea. But she had also made an herb tea from the green leaves, then poured it cool into a Coke bottle. She had a dime-store cork-bottom sprinkler top for it—didn't everybody?—and that's what she used to plug up the Coke bottle before shaking lemony scent onto clothes on the ironing board, dampening the cotton to relax it so she could iron it flat and smooth. All this was before permanent press and steam irons. Irene had used lemon verbena in pound cakes, lining the pan bottom with leaves. Not too many people got it to last through the winter, though. They'd plant it outside and forget to dig it up. Irene was always rooting cuttings and passing them along. She wondered if Sua Nag had any lemon grass uses like that, or if no grass, maybe she could use some verbena?

It was really hard to find words to talk to Sua Nag, but there had to be some way to communicate without them. She kept trying. She had such respect for the woman. Irene believed herself to be possibly the second-best sewing hand on the mezzanine; she believed the best was Sua Nag. Neither one of them was going to get a prize for it, and something usually got in the way of incentive, but it was how Sua Nag worked with honor. It was her integrity that impressed Irene, not just her "numbers." The way Sua Nag sewed, and did not waste time, it was as though she too, like Irene, was thinking of the men and women who would wear or bear this camo. She sewed as though she worked for the ones in the field as well as for those at home. Sua Nag sewed with passion, and Irene believed she sewed with love. It wasn't easy to care; it was easier to be good at something than glad at it. It was possible to earn incentive and not care at all. Irene had—like Sua Nag Vang—been observing without watching, and she did not judge her coworkers, but she measured them, because she was measuring herself as well. When you try to live up to a mark, one question to ask yourself might be, "how high?" but the other question is, "who drew it?"

Early in what Irene thought of as "the lemon squeeze" initiative, she had decided to sit near Sua Nag at lunch and just sort of mention gardening, grannies, or whatever. Apparently the end seat at the table, to Sua Nag's left two seats away, was way too close for Sua Nag, as she immediately moved down a chair and set up again. Irene asked her, "Does anyone ever call you Sunny?" There was a pause while Sua Nag looked at the far wall.

"No," she answered. They ate the rest of lunch without passing another word.

Somehow it seemed impossible to imagine how to bring up anything about lemon grass or verbena cuttings. "How 'bout that lemon grass!" Irene imagined saying. Nothing in life in general, in Sunday school, or at Happy Time had prepared her for this. She sat there feeling very much in the wrong place. There'd have to be another way to learn about lemon grass.

She waited while the tiny woman tidied up her things and left them on the table for her trip to the washroom. Irene, on a seemingly casual walk by, set a little jar of plum jelly with its label, "for Sua Nag," beside the lunch bag and kept on moving. She hadn't signed her name. Irene didn't stick around; she scooted through the double doors, turned right, and went down the whole length of the cutting floor, where she crossed to the outside wall and stairs, clocked in there, and went up to sew. Her heart raced as if she had committed a crime. It felt good.

A week later when she got back from lunch, right in the middle of her sewing chair was a perfect and anonymous cantaloupe in a grocery bag. She settled it in her tote bag, but she could smell it all afternoon. When she took it home, she told Deke about Sua Nag. "Somebody said she's Hmong," she told him. He knew all about them.

"They're heroes," he said quietly. "All of 'em."

After supper they went to the den and Deke checked e-mail, and then they each sent a message to Davy and also to Sherry and the kids. Deke

Googled "Hmong," and they sat together reading. Deke was studying war. What Irene got out of it was about the culture, the embroidery, and about the custom of not looking directly at another person. Also she saw that they preferred things fresh and were not great consumers of processed food or sugar. Now the plum jelly seemed like a terrible idea. Before she went to bed, she checked the calendar—waning moon, just what she needed—and stepped out onto the porch to clip some tender sprigs of new growth from the verbena. She put them in a pint jelly jar of water on the kitchen windowsill to root—this time maybe something the woman could actually use.

During the night Deke had bad dreams. He didn't do that much anymore. Researching what he called the Montagnards had upset him, stirred him up. The Hmong had been heroes. Every last one of them had death sentences on their heads from the Communists. They never fell, unless dead. Being that sort of hero is not something genetic; it is something they choose, something they do, a way of belonging to each other that makes the whole people "one body." Deke couldn't—or wouldn't—tell Irene what that body had done and what had been done to it, but he knew. Those thoughts kept him groaning all night in his sleep, like broken bones.

7

Over Labor Day weekend the newlyweds Link Purdy and his wife K'shaundra moved into the tenant house. They weren't going to work on shares. They were paying rent—had paid a month ahead and signed a contract Deke had printed off the Internet. Link was going to work for wages in town. He already had a job changing oil in trucks. K'shaundra was looking for work. Irene gave her a ride to Frazier on Tuesday. She'd had to wait, wait, wait in the yard, engine running, while K'shaundra got ready. They were almost late. Irene had told her she wouldn't have an interview today, just a chance to fill out the forms and turn them in. K'shaundra was ready for business. She was fully rigged out, looking her best. On the way Irene told her how to find the lobby, how to fill out the forms, and where to turn them in. "But the lobby won't open until 9:00 A.M.," Irene told her, "unless you have an appointment. Which you don't. And you can't come in with me." Since she'd have a couple of hours to kill, K'shaundra had wanted to drive on down to Hardee's and get a sausage biscuit. She surely did think that was a grand solution, but Irene had told her, no, there wasn't time.

K'shaundra decided to wait in the car, maybe sleep a little longer. She needed it. Moving day had just worn her down, she claimed. "Will you call me at fifteen minutes till nine?" she asked. She yawned. Irene had her cell number.

"I can't call. No cell phones in the building, I can't leave the building, and we don't have a phone on the floor."

K'shaundra looked around. She pointed. "Just stand in the door and holler. Just holler my name. I'll get up. I'm used to it," she said.

"I'll have Mr. Grayson call you, if I can get in to see him."

"Who?"

"My boss," Irene told her, "and maybe yours. What if they put you up on the mezzanine where I am, and he's your boss and knows you sleep in the parking lot and need a wake-up call?"

"Don't tell him I'm asleep in the car," she said, laughing. "Maybe he's calling me at work. Maybe this is my workplace. I'll be professional," she said. "I can do professional."

She asked Irene to leave the keys. "So I can work the windows." K'shaundra looked away. She looked sly, like she thought Irene was a fool. Maybe Irene was. Irene needed to think.

"Are you too hot or too cold?" Irene asked.

K'shaundra shrugged. "I just never know."

"It's not too cold now, and it won't be too hot before nine," Irene decided. She had to run to make it to the clock. K'shaundra said goodbye and thanks; she'd find her own way home if she wasn't right here at the car when Irene got off her shift. She had plans to meet a friend for lunch and was going to walk on the sidewalk to town. That's what she said, and it began to seem more real to her as she thought it through. "Don't you worry," she told Irene. Her friends—some friend—would drive her home to the farm "before Link even knows I'm missing." Irene set the electric windows, leaving them halfway. She didn't leave the keys.

In the days to come the Purdys just couldn't get settled in and down at the farm. Their honeymoon was about over. Something was always wrong. Once Link needed Deke to drive over and jump his dead battery. Another time they ran out of dog chow; when Deke ran by in his truck on the way back from the feed store and shoveled a bucket of Purina out to help them with the dog, three pit bull puppies tumbled out of the front door when Link answered Deke's knock. They had signed a "no indoor pet" clause in the renter's contract. "This is not good," Deke said. "You tellin' me," Link said. "They all bitches." That's when Deke noticed that Link had installed a satellite dish on the roof on the far side, just on the roof itself, no tar, no caulk, no flashing—had drilled it in, screwed it on, and there it was. By then it was payday, and their rent was two weeks late; Deke mentioned it. "Gotta get to the bank and get this thing cashed," Link explained. A week later K'shaundra knocked at the kitchen door, shy little taps. Irene was finishing up the supper dishes. Irene could smell beer. K'shaundra didn't step in. "I need to borrow some tampons," she said.

"I hoped you'd come to pay the rent," Irene told her. She invited the woman in, but K'shaundra waited on the porch. Irene pushed the door shut and went to speak to Deke. He was asleep in his chair. She went on down the hall for a moment and then returned and opened the door. K'shaundra was still there. She handed her the supplies. Irene had put a five-dollar bill in with them.

K'shaundra looked at Irene and flashed her wonderful eyes high beam. "Make that twenty and you'll never see me again," she promised. She lurched off the porch and went back across the grove to their house. Irene could hear her desolate laughter as she went.

Link was gone already, but Deke and Irene didn't know. K'shaundra moved out before Halloween, with not a word of notice or a cent of rent. They never saw the dogs again. There were some scuff marks from moving things out, and only one lightbulb was left; even the one in the refrigerator was gone. But the house wasn't trashed.

Irene rented a steamer at the market and cleaned the carpet in the front rooms. She always made things nice for whoever came next. While the carpet dried, she planted spring bulbs along the walk in front and around the cherry tree outside the kitchen window, so there would be daffodils to look at, for the one washing dishes. The autumn leaves were done, and she had raked them away, bagged them for compost. Deke was coming to pick her up in the truck. After she swept the front porch, she unfurled the runner she had brought to keep the carpet fresh. She had bought new mats at the dollar store, and she laid down a bright Welcome on each of the porches, front and back. Energy-saving fluorescent curly lightbulbs had been placed in the sockets and a regular one in the fridge. She had put a roll of paper towels on the holder in the kitchen and placed another on the sink in the bath, and there were new bars of hand soap in the lavatory and by the kitchen sink. She had hung a new plastic liner for the shower curtain. She had bought a wastebasket for the bathroom and a garbage can for the kitchen, with a liner in it and more liners in the kitchen drawer. There were some paper plates, cups, and picnic ware in the cabinet, along with a little set of salt and pepper. She had even provided a small bottle of dish soap.

When Deke came to pick her up, wrestle the carpet machine out to the truck, and walk through, he didn't say anything, not even about the expensive lightbulbs, but when he saw how she had folded the toilet tissue on its new roll into a fancy arrow point of professional hospitality, he stated, "This is not a hotel." A new broom and a mop stood behind the kitchen door with a matching dustpan. On the shelf over the washer and dryer she had placed a small bottle of laundry detergent and some dryer sheets in a sandwich bag. She had written out simple, clear instructions for the machines and taped them at eye level. All the miniblinds had been washed in the bathtub and rehung, adjusted to let light in but maintain privacy. The heat pump had a new filter. On a metal dish on the mantel there were matches next to a beeswax candle. She had lightly sanded the cedar lining in the hall closet, and from time to time as the furnace cycled on, a cedar-spice whiff would waft out. Without a stick of furniture in the house, it seemed cozy, blessed. All the windows and mirrors had been cleaned, and the refrigerator, in the light of its new bulb, looked almost new. The ice maker had a new filter. She had opened a fresh box of baking soda and put it in the freezer. She had put bottles of springwater on the top shelf. Now she dried out the sink so there would be no water marks, tied up the trash, and gathered the cleaning kit she was taking back, her everyday things. "Ready?" he asked, meaning, time to head for the truck, drop off the rug machine at the store in Ready, and then go home for supper.

"I think so," she said. He walked through, smiling. She smiled back. "I could be happy here." She had a little list, budget items or maybe

55

things they had at home. She'd look around. Maybe stop by Fred's. Coat hangers, she thought, and clothespins. She had some of those things. She would have liked to have a flashlight for the kitchen, a basic can opener, some duct tape, a hammer and two kinds of screwdrivers, pliers, picture nails, maybe scissors, a sewing kit, a chain of safety pins, and a little battery-operated travel-size alarm clock. It seemed to her that a house didn't feel "alive" unless time was ticking in it somewhere. Irene imagined a pretty kitchen towel and a fresh new pot holder. But maybe that could be in the welcome basket, with some fresh-baked bread and plum jelly.

She went on out to the yard, set the trash in the truck bed, and began loading the black bags of leaves. She had finished and was in the truck when Deke was done walking through, turning off lights and locking up. Deke had had the place rekeyed. He was swinging a tied-shut Food Lion bag, one of the spares Irene had stashed in the kitchen drawer. He put it gingerly on the floor behind his seat; it landed a little hard and made a telltale kind of clink. Deke grimaced. It surprised her very much what he had done, if she was right about what it sounded like. The thought deleted her growing shopping list and all words right out of her mind, as well as her mouth. They rode along in silence, and he knew she had figured it out: he had waited until she was in the yard, then had gone back through the house removing most of the lightbulbs. The longer their silence went on, the harder it was to break it. "We didn't take 'em to raise," he said, as though tenants were users and takers, so he took first, afraid of softness, of making things easy, and then she knew she was right; the bag was stuffed with confiscated lightbulbs. She never said a word about it. Not one "Do unto others" phrase or shamed sigh escaped her, but he had known her a long time. "I have been done unto," was all he said. He had to bring in the bag. She didn't offer, just slid down out of the truck and went on in and began getting supper ready. She simply couldn't think of anything to say. He set the bag on the shelf in plain sight in the utility room. For a few days she felt that they gave off some sort of bruising energy or odor; it affected her throat.

Irene and her Sunday school class had been praying that God would send them good and reliable tenants. She asked them to pray harder. She and Deke took the advice of folks who had been through it and knew: don't advertise in the *Messenger* or the Camden paper or website; just "ask around." No more total strangers with no references. Nothing noteworthy had happened so far. Not even a nibble.

K'shaundra had been hired at Frazier in shipping, not to sew. Different lunch times, different parts of the building, but sometimes their paths crossed. Irene stood in line behind her at the door one afternoon, clocking out. "Another day, another dollar," Coquita, the next one up to swipe, said and then shoved on out the door.

"You musta got a raise," K'shaundra hollered after her. She seemed happy.

In mid-November, K'shaundra stopped by the mezzanine lockers before first shift. She was way off from her own work station, and she had a request. She drew Irene aside. They stood there with backs turned to the work floor, and K'shaundra asked quietly if Irene would prefer to donate to the no-fault divorce fund by cash or check.

Prefer? Irene wondered, or rather marveled. K'shaundra drew a Planter's peanut jar from her peacoat pocket and shook it. Inside were small bills and coins—quarters, not nickels and dimes. There was a computer-printed label taped on, but Irene did not take time to read it.

"Tell me about it in a hurry," she insisted. "Maybe just skip to the—"

"It's no-fault," K'shaundra said. "I'm not blaming anybody."

"You can't do this," Irene told her.

"I'll tell him," she exclaimed.

"I mean, *here*. Frazier's got no soliciting." Irene shut her locker and turned to go. "I've gotta sew," she said.

"Maybe just five dollars?"

"How can that help?"

"It'll show you care," she replied.

For some reason, Irene burst out laughing. She reached into her apron pocket and felt around. She brought out a quarter and dropped it

57

in the jar. It hit the bottom hard. "Y'all may have to work things out," she said, still amused, and headed for her chair.

Just before Thanksgiving, Sua Nag tried to explain to Irene about Hmong New Year, which fell well before the calendar new year. In fact, it coincided with American Thanksgiving. It had something to do with rice, Irene figured, but the rest was just not getting through. Sua Nag, frustrated from knowing more than she could ever say—and didn't Irene know how that felt!—stared into her own locker on the Monday before turkey day and said, "You work compute?"

"Yes," Irene acknowledged.

"Yes, yes," Sua Nag agreed.

They stared into their lockers, side by side. "You work compute, Google Hmong happy new year!" Sua Nag told her.

Irene did, and that's how she found out about new year customs just in time to wish Sua Nag, "Eat 30!"

"Yes, yes," Sua Nag beamed, looking at her shoes.

Davy sent an e-mail for Thanksgiving and then called. Where he was the dinner for the troops was over, while Irene and Deke and the others were just beginning; they made digital photos to send later—close-ups of the turkey and casseroles and pies and relishes, and the kids at their little table and the rest of them. Every table leaf had been installed to make room and was covered with the ten-foot-long wedding damask Irene had inherited from her great-grandmother, who had created the "entre deux" tatting inserts herself. Davy's wife and children were there too; Sherry had driven down from Kentucky with her parents. Some of the men were going hunting, some weren't. Some of the women were talking about driving over to Dahlonega to the designer outlets just to look and maybe drive up to the Southern Living Designer Show House to see decorations. All the cousins were having breakfast with Santa on Saturday morning.

Irene understood why Davy's wife had come on down from Fort Campbell. It was going to be good to be together, but she knew that what Sherry also was doing was "trading off," so that at Christmas, when Davy flew home, he and his wife and children could truly be "home" for the holidays, Davy and Sherry's home, not riding up and down the highway, spreading him around. If family wanted to see him, they could travel to Kentucky. That was how Deke and Irene were planning it, to drive up and visit. Since Irene had not yet worked a full year at Frazier, she didn't get but five days of paid time off. She was holding on to them for that precious week of the holidays. Deke was driving them up Friday after Irene got off work. They'd drive through, and that would give them Saturday through the next Sunday. She could sleep on the way home, and if he had to drop her off at the plant in her road clothes, not even take her home, she was willing. She'd go through that for a glimpse, let alone a visit. Really, just for a glimpse. What mother wouldn't?

Irene remembered that road crew she had sat watching work last summer. They were machete-clearing brush and tractor bushhogging on the Camden highway. Traffic both ways was stopped by flagmen, while the driver of the tractor power-lifted the mower up to thresh its way along through overgrown ditch shrubs. The elderberries were blooming, and the mower flung the flower heads like bridal bouquets. The young man who had caught Irene's eye had leaped and caught flowers, and several motorists beeped their horns. The crew hollered. The mower was taking a long time. No one knew how long. Drivers who did not want to wait U-turned and headed back toward town, to detour by a different road. As Irene inched closer, she tried not to notice the workers on the crew, many without shirts on, working bare to the waist in the broiling sun, their white prison pants with blue stripes stark against their dark or tanned skin. What if that were Davy, Irene thought. Her heart lurched. *It would never be, never.* She knew that. But what if? Here she sat, looking at someone's son. His family would not get to see him that morning probably. Maybe they did not even know where he was. Some woman gave birth to that boy and had lost sight of him, for whatever reason. He did not seem ashamed or cowed. He seemed interested in his work. He was a young man doing manly things. He took over the flag then and was the one directing traffic. He helped the man on the tractor back out of the thicket and turn and jostle on down the shoulder to the next place he would cut. She could see the sweat on the young man's chest, the bits of green and twigs stuck there. She dreaded looking into his face, but it would be worse if she knew him; she required it of herself to look, brought her eyes up, as though she were looking for the sake of the mother who couldn't be there, or be blessed by the chance to see what she was seeing. She didn't know him. He wasn't looking at her of course. She wanted to report, *He seems happy. He looks well. He is a beautiful young man.* Would she have prayed for him that day, the mother who couldn't be there? Irene could do that much. She could pray for them both. Sometimes, most times, the world was too large for Irene, the list too long. Now all she said, as though she drew them forward by the hands, one on each side of her, "Here's two more."

The young man's voice had broken into her distraction. He was tapping on her window, and when she powered it down to hear, he said, "*Will* you just move?"

She had a chance to speak to him, but all she said was, "Yes," easing carefully into the oncoming lane as he flagged her by, safely past the mower and back into the right lane and on, the other cars following like obedient ducks.

There was a slight change of plans for the holidays, a big surprise for Irene. Deke got a call from Davy at the airport. He had gotten an earlier flight, a whole day earlier, and they cooked up Plan B. Deke would drive to Atlanta, pick up Davy, drive him to Ready, take him by the plant, and just knock Irene's socks off. They'd spend the night at the farm, and in the morning Davy would drive Deke's truck to Kentucky. When Irene and Deke went up for Christmas the next week, they'd go in the car, and coming home Deke would drive his truck back and Irene would drive her car. This was their Christmas gift, this time alone with him. Of course, Deke had already called Jenny and Tonya, and they were bringing supper, barbecue from Sonny's. Davy wouldn't need the truck after Christmas; he and Sherry had a van. Plus, in the new year everybody who could would be gathering in Georgia in February, meeting at the airport in Atlanta, the entire clan mustering to see Davy off as he headed back to his new duty station in Afghanistan. Or they'd all go to Fort Campbell again if he was flying out from there. By then Irene would have earned eight more hours of personal time off.

Plan B was going to work out for Tonya too. She had a special gift in mind for her brother and Sherry. "Don't scream a word," she texted Sherry. "Damn if U tell mom."

"Come on," Sherry replied.

Tonya was up to something. "Gift card. Visa prepaid. On its way today."

"What?" Sherry texted.

"Only good for one thing," Tonya typed. "PROMISE."

"?"

"SWEAR."

"Hint?"

"What JFK Jr and bride did on honeymoon."

"!"

"No," Tonya typed. "Tats."

"Tats? Where?"

"Contstamapole or something."

"Turkey?"

"Turky? No way."

"Way. Cnstnpl iz N Turkey."

"Where tats?"

"Tats where it iz." Tonya could play this game all day.

"CALL ME NOW." Sherry texted, fit to be tied.

The first word Sherry yelled was, "Where?"

"I'm not askin' you to go to Constnattin Friggin Turkey to get tattoos," Tonya said. "They are bound to have a parlor in Kentucky. Or you could come here. That's where we got ours."

Sherry gave it some thought. "You saying that you and Brad got tattooed?"

"It's adorable," Tonya answered. "We match." She sent the photo.

Sherry looked, looked away, looked back. Couldn't read it. Too small.

Tonya said. "It's private."

"JFK Jr. and his bride?" Sherry asked again.

"Shamrocks of course."

"Where?" Sherry wondered. "And if you say Turkey one more time I am going to tell your Momma and Daddy what you and Brad have been up to. And I am going to lie."

"Oh," Tonya said. She knew she'd won. They were going to do it! She had known the moment she thought of it. Perfect. "Y'all can do it at Christmas. People are. All over. Roseanne did. And—"

"For the last time," Sherry said, "where? And I don't mean Rose-anne. And I don't mean Constantinople."

So Tonya told her.

Deke didn't tell Irene a word about Davy's call. Davy was in Gander, but there was a layover. He could get a flight to Atlanta if he bought his own ticket, and that's what he decided to do. That money was going to be for their present, anyway. His kit would go on through to Fort Campbell; he could claim it there. He'd look kinda rough, he warned his father. "Just as I am," he said, rubbing the fresh beard on his weathered cheek. "Will that do?"

Deke replied, "I owe you some change, buddy." Then he told Irene he had to go to the VA for his annual physical, had a chance to get that done because somebody canceled and he would take that slot and see her at suppertime. He made a few phone calls.

Irene went to work just as if it were any ordinary day of her life. She did wonder about the decorations going up at Frazier; lots of folks on the crew, and they seemed to be in a hurry. Everybody always toured the plant through those doors, good place for the photo op, which is why—besides worker morale—there was always a banner or something to fire them up and on. Plus the flag on the wall. Maybe some bigwigs, she thought when she saw them attaching the yellow bows; she hadn't read Wednesday's *Messenger*. And nothing had been said in last week's

"Communication Meeting" on the mezzanine. She'd probably never know; visitors didn't usually come upstairs. She surely couldn't see a thing from where she sat except people sewing.

The bridge and companionway were being decorated with repurposed bell tower bunting from the Fourth of July. Ellen in Front End had the garment steamer smoothing it down; it was being looped up with massive yellow ribbon bows by Ginger in Audit. The matrix-dot banner had been unfastened from the railing—FRAZIER PRIDE SUPPORTS OUR TROOPS—and moved to the wall below the flag, centered—more shouting and arm waving—and taped on. The place was a madhouse; they had to use the other stairs. Irene was sewing again after lunch when somebody hollered. Then there was a commotion downstairs, and Irene thought someone had fallen or dropped something important, but it and more shouting went on, and some part of her harked, because this was a factory, and on the second floor there was always something to be concerned about, especially fire; she paused and listened for the Klaxon to sound, in case they had to make an emergency response. Her mind tracked the escape routes. She could find her way in the dark. Maybe they were testing the alarm system. Sometimes they were repairing it. Maybe the squirrels had chewed the wires on the roll-up doors again. Or there was another skunk; skunk day had been something else: there had been screaming, a stampede. She stopped sewing now—and she never stopped sewing—to ask, "What is going on?" They couldn't smell skunk, or smoke. Kit said, "They never tell us anything up here. I'm going to go see," and she did. Coquita was sure it was a skunk or a snake: "Ah hope ta hell runs the other way. Ah got nothin' to throw."

Betty, walking up, caught Coquita coming back from her locker. She had retrieved a little keychain canister in its holster and was shoving it into the grenade pocket in her fatigues. "Coquita, don't tell me you think pepper-spraying a skunk is a good idea?"

"Might be a snake."

There had been a young copperhead in the corner of Mrs. Champion's office last year. It had been ruled a natural event and not an act of sabotage or disgruntlement. Now what difference would that make to the snake or the person it bit? Betty considered. "First of all, how close do you want to get?" Before Coquita could answer, Betty handed Irene the note she had been sent to deliver from Mr. Grayson. Irene had to read it twice. Irene was being summoned downstairs. Main lobby. Betty didn't know why. She just knew something was going on.

Kit came back, didn't sit, grabbed Coquita, and said, "Come *on.*" They headed for the stairs. They walked right by JaNice, who didn't have a chance to say, "No way." She went after them, answering her phone.

"Is it the president?" Irene wondered.

Betty warned, "Don't start a panic!" But she drafted along also. Word about what was going on spread fast. Irene was the only one who didn't have a clue. By the time Irene was on the bridge and heading down the companionway steps, half the sewing floor was heading after her, including Mr. Grayson and Sua Nag.

Irene didn't understand. She thought it must be a general emergency, so she began to walk faster, almost at a trot. She could hear them behind her. All around her, workers were standing, looking at the oncoming crowd, looking at Irene, but she did not notice this. She started to push open the glass door at the end of the long hall, but Jacky opened it for her and bowed her through. The acoustics were different here—a lower ceiling, closer walls, a kind of hush and step-down from the hive in production. Irene almost paused when she saw the crowd in the lobby. She saw Mr. Frazier and Mrs. Champion. She saw all of them looking her way, and someone with a camera. Then she saw Deke. He was not upset; he was holding steady; he was smiling. He stepped forward, toward her, and then she saw Davy. He was in battle dress, rumpled and road tested, jet lagged and caffeine jazzed. He more or less scooped her up, extinguished her against himself. She was beating on his broad back, as far around him as she could reach. Not sobbing, just beating. She couldn't hurt him. It felt like he had on armor. He was strong from carrying a soldier's burdens.

Mr. Frazier told her, "Go on back and show him off, troll him on through, then y'all just go on home, the three of you, and let us get back to work. Irene, I don't want to see you until—" he consulted his watch, enjoying himself—"next year." Then they were stepping through the double doors—"Did he say next year?" she asked Deke—into the factory. Kit got Irene's lanyard and ran upstairs, retrieved her jacket and purse, and helped her shove her rubbery arms into the sleeves. It was like putting socks on a sleeping baby. For Irene, none of it seemed real. She couldn't think what to do. She stood there watching Davy. Her boy was moving through the workers, shaking hands. "You know my mama?" he asked over and over, marveling, as if they were the ones who had come from a far country. Kit finally gave up on Irene, took the lanyard back, ran to the break-room time clock, and swiped her out. "I know that's illegal, so shoot me." She saluted the security camera, handed Irene's lanyard and purse to Deke, and said, "You caint push a string! Drag her out of here." Finally, they went, one time only, first time ever: fire exit, mid-building. Coquita kicked the door open, reared back, and used her boot on the bar; Kit held it, backing it open with her butt and standing there, all the alarms blaring, while Irene and Deke and Davy went home.

"I would vote for him," Coquita said as they hiked upstairs and tried to settle back to work. "And I do not vote easy for any *man*."

It was a glorious Christmas. The family took digital videos with a new camera. They took photos by the hundreds, including of each other taking photos. Irene and Deke were sitting at their own dining table in January, a month before Davy deployed to Afghanistan, sorting pictures and trying to organize them into themes. Right in the center was one of Davy and the baby blowing out the candle on the baby's first birthday cake. Chocolate frosting was everywhere. The cake was almost bald.

Irene got up and went to the kitchen to make some coffee. There was a shy knock at the door, on the glass, one knuckle. Irene remembered that knock. She pulled the curtain back and looked into K'shaundra's face. She switched on the light, opened the door. The hen Mercy shook and flew down like it was morning, and when Irene invited K'shaundra in, Mercy came in too. Walked right in.

"I'm alone," she said when Irene looked past her and around. She wasn't looking for hens.

"How alone?" Irene wanted to know.

"We didn't divorce," K'shaundra told her, "if that's what you're asking."

"Because?" Irene questioned. She gathered Mercy, took her back out, set her in the crate, came back in, and switched off the light. She patted the table.

"You know we never married." K'shaundra sat down.

"Oh." Irene washed her hands and dried them on a blue-checked towel, hung it back on the dishwasher door handle, and touched it to make the pattern even. "And?"

"He had a wife," she said. "Way off somewhere. I couldn't marry with him."

"But you knew that, right? That wasn't a lie on you."

"I did know," K'shaundra admitted. She must also have known this was coming. She handed back the quarter Irene had donated to the divorce jar. Irene took it, dropping it in a cup on the windowsill. "New project under way," K'shaundra announced. "Plan C?"

"K'shaundra, if you don't need a divorce, what do you need?"

"I want to rent. I want to stay at your place till next summer, maybe. Maybe until next year this time. Maybe just stay here, keep on staying."

"Why?"

"Link's going to jail and he's going to be gone and I know I'll be safe. I like this place." She looked around.

Irene poured coffee, poured each of them a mug. Deke had walked from the other room, had come to stand in the doorway to drink his.

"I think K'shaundra wants to rent our little house," Irene told him.

"It's empty," Deke agreed. "How can you afford it?"

"I'm steady workin'," she answered. "I'm through my ninety days."

"If someone *exactly like you* came to your door and asked you what you are asking us, what would you tell her?" Deke sipped coffee but kept his eyes on her over the rim. Finally she looked away.

66

"I'd tell her what I tol' Link: 'Some things just don't cut it after while.'"

"What if the girl at your door told you she was sorry?" Deke asked. "Said she was going to pay the back rent?" Irene turned away to the sink, watching their reflections in the window. She tapped the grounds from the filter cup and rinsed it and put it back in place. She got the cookie jar and handed each one of them a tea cake and a napkin. She was thinking, *This is what it is to be grown-up. We're grown-up now. We're all adults here.* It seemed to her that Deke was more grown-up than she was. She pulled out a chair and sat at the table and hoped Deke would sit down with them too, but he didn't.

Finally K'shaundra said, "I'm strongly sorry."

"What if he comes back?" Irene asked.

"He will," Deke stated.

"I'll practice," K'shaundra said. "I *been* practicing."

"What about some night he stops by and he's been walking in the rain because his car's broken down and he's soaked through and just wants to talk to you, rest a little, just get warm. Maybe he's got a bad cough and a fever."

"He's got a motorcycle now."

"That a fact?" Deke commented, then waited.

"He's going on trial. He's going up. He can't win; they've got witnesses." The whites of her eyes were very white. "Not me," she clarified.

"When is the trial?"

"Next week. Atlanta. It's federal. There's a lot bad wrong ain't gonna be fixed."

"You have to testify?"

"It was before my time." She considered. Then she explained, "I'm not implicated."

"Rent's the same," Deke said, "but you'll have to pay something more each time, till the back rent is paid up."

K'shaundra answered, "Will I?" She rubbed her forehead, figuring.

"Well, that's the question, isn't it?"

Irene asked, "Do you have any furniture?"

"We haven't signed any papers here," Deke warned her. He set his mug on the table. It was empty.

"How much do I owe you?" K'shaundra asked, as though it were the first time the thought had crossed her mind.

Despite every warning flag, they agreed. Friends helped her move in. One pickup truck load was it. K'shaundra wanted the contract changed to allow her—to require her—to pay rent every two weeks, payday to payday. She signed the contract "K'shaundra Purdy." She explained, "He was using my name. I won't be using his."

"We must be out of our minds," Deke said. A week had passed. "I never see a light over there," he realized. K'shaundra always parked around back, out of sight from the road. The front porch light stayed off, and there was nothing on the front porch or in the yard—no ornament, no chair. It was bleak. The blinds always looked the same. It appeared as though no one was living there. At first they thought it might have been from caution until Link's trial was over. They had no way to know how that was going. But if it was a budget thing, was she keeping the furnace off too, to shave a bit more off expenses to keep on paying them the back rent? Had she even paid to have the power turned on?

They thought about that, talked about that some during supper, and later Irene gathered up a quilt, a tote with cans of soup, some cookies, packets of cocoa mix, a handful of tangerines, a jar of her bread-and-butter pickles, some peanut butter, a sprinkling of candies, a box of crackers, and some cheddar cheese. Deke went to the utility room and got that Food Lion bag of lightbulbs, in case that was why she was in the dark. Deke had his key. If she wasn't home, they were just going to set the things inside the door.

They drove down the grove lane and eased over the berm onto the long barn access, then back around by the little house and to the front again and parked, headed out. Her car was in back. She didn't respond when Irene called her name. Deke knocked, knocked again louder, and then announced he was going to use his key, which he did. They couldn't see her at first, dark against the dark paneling in a dark room.

She was sitting on the carpet, her legs scissored straight out, her back flat against the wall. She was facing the door. They heard her breathing, snuffling through a bloodied nose. They must have just missed him. Maybe he fled when he saw their lights coming as they circled through the grove. If Link left heading back toward the bypass, he had not gotten far. Deke flipped on the lights, and K'shaundra begged him to turn them off again. He didn't. He switched on the floods front and back on the porches and went out to the truck and got his pistol. While he was out there, he called 911. When he came back in, he slid the burglar chain into its channel. He walked through the house putting bulbs in where they were missing, leaving them burning. No windows were broken. "How'd he get in?" The knob lock had been pushed in. She'd have had to open it from the inside. Deke wondered if she had given him a copy of the new key.

K'shaundra was down but hadn't fallen. She seemed to have slid, like she was still standing where he had thrown her against the wall before he left and just let herself go. True. She knew if she fell he'd finish her, kicking. Link was a kicker. He had killed with his boots. Or let her believe it, stopping just short. Part of his art. Something broke in her this time besides ribs. Something like chains. Irene was kneeling beside her, offering her a wet cloth, talking, listening.

"My fault," K'shaundra told them. "I got so tired being careful, tired taking advice."

"He won't do it again," Irene stated.

"Did he get anything?" Deke looked around the empty rooms.

"Me," she said. "Next time I'll kill him," she vowed.

Irene said, "No!"

"Don't worry," K'shaundra assured them. "I'll get him out in the yard," as though it was a matter of blood on the carpet.

They raised her to her feet. She could stand.

"I thought he was going to prison," Irene said.

"Next week," K'shaundra replied. "Judge has the flu."

8

By the end of March, their "strike soldier" was in Afghanistan, K'shaundra's rent was almost caught up, the wild plums along the creek were already setting fruit, and the martin scouts had come and inspected the nest sites and flown to fetch the others. Deke and Brad had the poles back up, the gourds ready since February. There were bluebirds in the houses along the line fence trail on Dutton Road. That had been Davy's Eagle Scout project. A wren had built a nest in the grapevine wreath on the door at church. Barn swallows were mudding up their nest walls on the back porch light, and Deke was already saying he couldn't see why they'd put up with that again—just what he always said. The early jonquils had started the season along the pasture fence almost a month ago, and now the paperwhites were blooming on the sunny banks. The heavy part of calving season had begun. The pastures would be green by the time the calves could eat it.

The water in the pond was still deep cold when Irene took a printout of some of her computer research to work. She had found pictures of carp, bream, bass, and catfish. She had some photographs of the farm and a map. She had already given Sua Nag cuttings of lemon verbena and had shown her the photograph of her great-grandmother in the oval frame, the one where she was a baby in that wicker carriage and Irene's great-great grandfather and great-great grandmother were standing so still and stiff, their eyes fixed on a far view, holding steady for the long exposure. There was a date on the photograph: 1907. One by one Irene had dealt the other photos down, generation by generation, showing that little baby's life and finally showing Irene in the picture when she had arrived on the family tree. In one she and her granny were holding hands. Irene showed Sua Nag one with the family lined up on the porch of the unpainted house, with the various buckets and containers of "pretties"—pass-along plants her great-granny had collected through friendship and visits and gifts and ditch rescues. One showed the very bucket of verbena Sua Nag's cutting had come from. Irene had taken a photo of it on her own porch last fall, and then a view of the house from across the road. Even at that distance, you could tell that verbena was really something. It was on wheels; it had to be. Somehow Irene had been able to get all that across—or thought she had—without looking anybody in the eye or waving her hands or speaking loud or otherwise making a fool of herself or unwittingly insulting Sua Nag in particular or the Hmong in general.

Sua Nag, in return, had brought Irene the only photograph she had of ancestors: a modern snapshot of her husband's grandfather and their whole family bank fishing at Pines Creek the first summer they came to the United States. The old man was wearing a suit, as though he was on his way to church, or thought fishing was holy. He had on a straw hat and sunglasses, and Irene could not really see his face. He was looking away from the camera and had a good-looking right ear. Sua Nag and Mr. Vang and their children? Yes, yes, Sua Nag nodded, three children, all grown now. Irene had already shown her a photograph of Deke and their three children, all grown now.

Irene had given this relationship some thought. She hoped one day she could learn some Hmong words. And she hoped that Sua Nag could learn more English ones. But until then she trusted that Sua Nag could understand more than she could speak back. After all, she was a naturalized citizen. Sua Nag had a driver's license and could read directions for all sorts of things and newspapers; Irene had seen her looking at newspapers—not just the pictures or sale ads—left on the table in the break room. They sat together at lunch, and in the space between them at the long table, their backs to the TV, Irene spread out her and Deke's latest idea, pages in order, a list to go down to be sure she made her

71

points and that Sua Nag could read later and mark the ones she did not understand. She walked Sua Nag through the idea. What it all boiled down to, really, was maybe. Maybe the Vangs would like to come to the pond and fish? "No charge," Irene said. "We won't bother you. Welcome anytime." She showed the printouts of the fish and made hand measurements of their usual sizes. She didn't think the carp were good to eat; she wasn't sure. But they weren't dangerous to humans who didn't scare easily. She didn't think Sua Nag did. She thought they would like the way the hossy carp snorted and guzzled, their little eyes staring up sleepy and full of their own possibilities, like a baby at the breast.

The map Deke had drawn for the Vangs had the access lane off their back drive highlighted in green. He had drawn a little car on the map, to show where to park. There were some trees and shade.

There was one gate with a padlock. Deke had the key copied. He had drawn that pipe gate on the map, and the little padlock was circled in blue. He had chosen a blue blank for the copy of the key. He wanted to put it on a ring, but Irene had explained to him about the keys on Sua Nag's lanyard. Irene wasn't sure how to convey this part, but she pointed to the key, held up her own lanyard, and then pointed to the outline of the key on the map with the arrow to the blue circled padlock. "For you. Anytime."

Sua Nag kept on looking at the photographs. She touched the one of the long shot of the farm and pond. The cattle were off in a far field that day, and of course the lane was between fences. The fences were to protect the wheat, not the cows. "Wheat, not pasture," Irene explained. Sua Nag said, "Yes, yes."

"The cattle don't come to the pond," Irene told her. "They drink from the creek down there." The dam was fenced off. The chicken house was on the other side of the road, beyond the hill, nowhere near the creek. Sometimes it smelled pretty funky, but generally, even on days when the trucks came to clear out the broilers and haul them away and clean the house and lay down the new sawdust, the smell didn't oppress. Deke had planted pines and other evergreen windbreaks, and they had exhaust fans drawing the air the other way, into the cedars.

"No bull?" Sua Nag asked, looking at the photo of the cows way off. They rented one. He arrived in a trailer, created a sensation among the cows, did his work, and was gathered back up again into the trailer and driven away like a sultan to his next harem. This made sense, in bloodline ways, was safer, and kept it really easy to schedule calving.

"No bull," Irene agreed.

Sua Nag offered her hand and Irene laid the key in it.

"This big deal," she stated.

"Baby steps," Irene replied.

Sua Nag liked that. "Baby steps," she repeated.

Coquita breezed by, headed for the clock. She rapped a nicotined fist on the table as she passed. "Time to sew, ladies," she said. "Tea party's over."

The first time the Vangs came to fish, it was April. Sua Nag came to the house and knocked at the door. Irene was at the grocery store. Deke had been practicing. "*Nyob zoo,*" he said. He had about given up on *nyob*, but his *zoo* sounded a lot more like *zyhawn* than it used to. Sua Nag held out her right hand, palm flat, like half an applause, and wavered it for "so-so." Deke didn't scare her; they had met in town, but she had not come to visit. She showed him his own map like a ticket. She wouldn't come in. The others were in the car waiting, vigilant but not looking. Sua Nag held up the blue key. "OK?"

"Yes, yes," Deke said.

"Baby steps," she told him, heading for the car.

When Irene came home, Deke walked her to the stairs; she followed him up. The attic door wasn't locked. There was enough room to walk through the stacked cartons and bins. From there they could see the pond. There they all were, two in folding lawn chairs and one on a turned-over drywall bucket, and no fishing going on at all. Just old Mr. Vang in his straw hat and sunglasses, his grandson, and Sua Nag. Sitting there, backs to the world, looking at the water, avoiding the world's eye, catching some rays.

Strangely, mysteriously, but not for the first time, Deke astonished Irene, left her speechless. They stood side by side, his arm around her shoulders, hers around his waist, watching the Vangs through their attic window. Deke sniffed. No noise, just tears. "This was a good idea," was all he said.

At their lockers the next morning Sua Nag said, "Nice, but you need get duck."

Irene thought about it. There were wood ducks in winter, but they flew on. There was a Canada goose once. There were coyotes, but someone had told them to put a donkey in the pasture and the coyotes would stay away. They did, and they hadn't lost a calf since.

"Maybe ducks," Irene said. She'd ask Deke what he thought.

"Papa Vang bring give duck," Sua Nag said.

So that's how all that got started. No one knew where the gray geese came from. Irene could tell these were not the kind of ducks you name. Papa Vang liked duck soup.

Irene was down along the creek, thinking about what they might do with the tax refund while she was picking plums from the sunny side. She had walked the creek, harvesting the easy ones, and had not yet reached the turn-back point. She was saving room in her bucket for the ones she saw on the way back. It was a clear evening, warm, with a blue sky. The wheat had about another month till harvest; the field was strong and green. The breeze would move across it like a hand; she loved to watch it. From time to time cars or a truck went by. She heard them, but the road wasn't visible; it ran atop the hill. As the evening came on, the sun cast shadows of the unseen vehicles on the trees she stood among. That or something else caught her attention, as though she had heard her name. When she looked up, she saw two trucks and a car. The trucks had driven across the center line and across the oncoming lane to park at angles on the margin. They were headed the wrong way, so that was odd. The sun was low enough that she couldn't tell the color of the vehicles; they were in silhouette. Then a sedan came into view, parked like the trucks. Doors opened, and men got out. She recognized Deke and realized that the other truck must be Brad's. They didn't shut the doors; just came to the edge of the hill, stepped through the barbed wire fence, and started down through the wheat toward her. There were two people in the car, and they came on also. She set her plum bucket down.

Were they crazy, wading through the wheat like that? Four abreast, not in a row to minimize the damage? Sometimes when there is a hawk near, the hens hush, vanish, or hunker down as if they know what's good for them. It is instinct. Everything goes still while the shadow passes over. Irene had such an instinct; the sound left the film of her life, and in that warning silence a moment when she could have run. Something in her wanted to run. There was a fire in her chest, in her throat, challenging her to run and keep on running. If she kept on running, whatever the threat was it couldn't gain on her or bring her to the ground.

They were closer now; they had walked down the hill far enough that they were not silhouetted against that perfect sky. They came on, stirring life up, grasshoppers lifting into the light, settling back into the dark, with each step.

He already knows. Whatever it is, he already knows. At least he already knows, Irene thought. *Deke knows. I don't have to tell him.*

It couldn't be held against her, her wanting to run; the struggle against it was tremendous, was wearing her out. How suddenly tired she was. How she longed to lie down, as a woman in labor lies down to give birth. What a wonderful thought, "to give birth." To give. Birth. She had given. She had given birth. And now she was going to have to take. She was going to have to take death. She dropped to the earth, lay vanished in the wheat. She rested, between the pangs of taking death. But Irene couldn't take death lying down. She rolled over, face to the ground, and gripped handfuls of wheat, right at the roots, holding on as though some tearing wind was about to blow her away. She got up, first to a squat, still holding on to the wheat. Then she balanced on one hand and rose. She was standing it. She could see their faces now, recognizing Brad and Deke and memorizing the two strangers; she could see the glint of metal and medals on their dress uniforms. The cloth looked black in shadow. Her face was in sunlight from the nose up to the crown of her head. Like a mask of light. Like someone drowning in darkness.

Old Mr. Vang, his grandson, and Sua Nag heard it, that one piercing shrill cry against death, like an eagle's scream.

They had been arrayed along the bank of the pond, watching the ducks. From where they were, they could see the road, could see the trucks and then the car careen across and park crazy on the shoulder. One by one they had turned to watch, then got up and stood. They stood watch. They were a long way off, and it was almost sundown. They could see the four men coming across the field. They watched Irene vanish, like a magician's assistant, into the green as the men came on. They saw her rise again. They heard that shrill cry. They had heard that cry before, in another country. It wasn't an eagle then either.

9

May 3, 2011
Soldier's Remains Return Home
Journal-Constitution Staff

ATLANTA—In remembrance and honor of Staff Sergeant David G. Morgan, Governor Sonny Perdue has directed that the United States flag and the State of Georgia flag be flown at half-staff from sunrise to sunset on Monday, May 3.

Morgan, 29, of Ready, was killed by enemy fire April 21 while leading his rifle squad in fighting near Kunar in Afghanistan. He was a strike soldier with the 2nd Battalion, 502nd Infantry Regiment, 2nd Brigade ("Strike") Combat Team, 101st Airborne Division (Air Assault) of Fort Campbell, Kentucky.

A funeral and burial service for Morgan are planned for Monday at 3:00 P.M. at Pines Chapel Baptist Church on Dutton Road in Ready.

Morgan's remains were returned to Fort Campbell, Kentucky, on April 29 from Dover, Delaware. The remains will be flown back to Georgia today, arriving at the Camden Tri-State Airport at 10:15 A.M. The Georgia National Guard, law enforcement, and fire department personnel will participate in the arrival ceremony.

An hour before Davy's plane was scheduled to land in Camden, law enforcement and fire personnel in Ready were on task. Ready's motorcycle unit—which consisted in fact of one man and one bike—was stationed at the city limits, to thread the hearse safely through the three-way intersection. There were blue lights already flashing at the bypass, slowing folks down, officers ready to halt oncoming traffic and direct the cortege down Main. Every side street, every driveway would be blocked. Another patrol car waited at the Hardee's light to stop traffic and guide the procession onto Old Pines Road. The Forest Service fire truck waited where Old Pines vee'd into Dutton. Then three miles unpoliced until the driveway to Pines Chapel, where National Guard and the Legion created a living gateway, but for those three miles, every mailbox had a yellow ribbon and a flag. Cell phones kept everyone in touch. The air was filled with flying messages. Some of the Legion were at Tri-County, in Camden, watching for the plane. So were some of the Guard. Pines Chapel didn't have a large parking lot; blue gravel smoothed down with crusher run could hold maybe the first seventy cars. From what the Legion had heard on the phone, they would be needing more room. They voted on the west field beyond the church. It had been mowed that morning by volunteers from the Men's Class— Deke's pals—and with landscaper's paint they began marking off a traffic lane and boundaries.

The Women's Class had the church open and aired, and would close the windows and turn on the air-conditioning at 11:00. Food had already been delivered to the kitchen and more was coming, enough for an army. Coffee makers were set up and ready to be switched on. Someone was back there now halving lemons and making lemonade. Sweet tea and unsweetened were ready in ranks of gallon jugs. The portable freezer borrowed from Hardee's was full of ice.

Why were they doing all this? Because it was all they could do, and it kept them busy, and together. One of the younger women, Debby Bridge, stood in a hall door watching Beatrice Haney straighten a candle on the table in the sanctuary. The table had been moved to the side, at an angle, to leave room for the casket when it arrived. The Bible was open, and there was a cross but no flowers on the table. Later there would be plenty of flowers. Bea changed out the bookmark from purple to white with gold silk fringe. When she entered the hall, Macia

Gordon said, "A lot of folks going to be standing outside, I've just got a feeling. Have to leave the doors open." They didn't have a PA system or any need, before, for overflow seating or parking.

"This is for the front row," Bea said. "Their turn. They have to hear it. They need every word. The rest of us, we're here for them."

In Camden, Davy's plane was late and was going to be later, perhaps an hour, perhaps two or more. The message passed along the roads, cell by cell. People had begun parking where they could and waiting, all along the eighteen miles between Camden and Ready at every little settlement, church lot, turn lane, and store. Sooner or later they got word about the delay. Some had to go home; some had to pick up kids from preschool. Most came back. More arrived. When the school buses ran and Davy's plane had not landed yet, parents brought the children and stood along the route. The sidewalks in Ready began to fill. The crowds grew. Frazier Fabrics had closed in Davy's honor for the day, all day shifts. When afternoon began to wane and Davy's plane was still delayed, Frazier canceled the second shift also. Some people had brought chairs. Others sat in their cars or on tailgates. Still others sat on jackets on the grass. Infants napped in adult arms. Toddlers sat on their daddies' shoes. Pigeons on the roofs flew up, circled, and settled again. There were hundreds of flags. As the wait grew longer, it also grew shorter; no one was going home. People in houses along the route opened their kitchens, their bathrooms, their porches. The librarian brought out chairs, even the little ones for children, and set them on the lawn. Outside the nursing home, wheelchairs were lined up. From time to time an attendant backed a chair up, wheeled it inside, then brought it back again. Some citizens had begun to climb the fire escapes and perch along the rooftops. The newspaper staff already had a roof-top tripod set up, wind-braced, aimed south. Another photographer walked at ground level, making candid shots. No one could see as far as they wanted, and everyone kept looking, even though they knew, from the cell phones and word of mouth, that the plane hadn't even landed yet. Mimi's customers kept their eyes on the windows. Mimi had canceled all permanent waves because the ladies just couldn't let direct sun hit that lotion, and she knew they would jump up and run out. It was all just cut and dry for Mimi. This was her fifth war, the last one, she hoped. But she watched the mirror; Sergeant David Morgan wasn't going to get past her.

Every person along that route had a story. Everyone was part of the story. Everyone knew only part of the story. Everyone had a different perspective and motives. There was no explanation, really, for what was going on, for what was coming to pass. The editor of the *Messenger*—when it began to look as though nobody was forsaking the vigil—made some phone calls, and after that there was a helicopter from the Toccoa station bringing that perspective also. News at eleven. If then. If not, then whenever. "For the duration" began to take on new meaning for the pilot of the news 'copter. Before he would get the video he had been sent to record, he would have to return to home base and refuel. What he reported then, before he even began his story, brought more people to Ready, to line the way.

No one knew how late the flight bringing home Davy's body was going to be, so they stayed. Through speculation and rumor, cell phone to cell phone, various versions of how and why passed along the groups lining the roads—it might be past afternoon, might even be "on toward dark." When the afternoon train came along, no faster than a man's easy walk, gently hooting at the open Norfolk Southern grade crossings, the pedestrians caught up children and held fast. Little fists waved their flags now that something was happening. But that was all that was happening. "Do you think the plane has even taken off?" someone asked, and that question made its way along the ranks. Faces scowled up at the clouds.

In Camden, Irene had more time than usual to watch her family interact. Tonya and Brad and their kids, Jeff and Penny, were sitting in an L of leatherette using the coffee table in the first-class lounge as their work surface for crayons, games, and one of those puzzles with pieces shaped like the states, cut out of wood. Tonya was playing UNO with Jenny and Kev's crew; they were a bit older, past the coloring book stage. Jeff had already turned the map puzzle over so the names and colors were hidden and had worked it upside down and backward. Then he too played UNO. Irene didn't see a thing to fret about, but she kept looking over. They were not making a lot of noise, and this whole room had been closed off, just for them. When Penny held up a square piece of the map, Brad said, "Mmm, could be Colorado. But it could be Wyoming too." Irene glanced again. Jenny and Kev were still sitting back-to-back like bookends, facing different directions. Kev had pulled his chair out of line and made a little gap between him and the others, working on his laptop. He had a paper due in one of his classes.

Irene stood, stretched, and took a little walk around the waiting room. She gathered empty snack wrappers and remnants of cold coffee in paper cups, and put the trash in one of the bins. It seemed natural, not planned, when she cut back to the group in front of Kev's screen. He was typing, fast but intermittently, as though he was thinking something up. He didn't even look up until Irene said, "Just read me one sentence. One. I promise to be fascinated no matter what." Kev's topic—by now they all knew it—was "Beyond Kriedler: Lesson Plans for Peace-building in the Middle Schools." Kev didn't like the topic anymore, or middle schools much; if he had his druthers he'd be done with the classroom. He was still teaching two classes a day plus serving as assistant principal. Kev had sights on full principal or, better yet, a life in the quiet golden light of the pigeon-haunted old courthouse at the county office, administering from behind—as he imagined it—a vintage dark oak partners desk, with an assistant to screen his calls, maintain his calendar, and—if he could get that job before his Ph.D.— help him format his dissertation. He rubbed his face with both hands and focused on Irene. He looked tired. Nobody had had much sleep. She thought about telling Kev what the eye doctor had told her when she had gone to see if bifocals would help when she was working at the clock factory, close-focusing all day. "Every hour, lift your eyes and look off, look as far off as you can see." But she could tell that Kev already was focused on something far off. Kev's beard had already grown out enough to audibly scratch his hand as he rubbed his chin. He did not seem to understand what Irene was saying, as though she were speaking in a foreign tongue. She patted his shoulder, walked on back to Deke, and sat again. He flipped his cell phone shut and shook his head. No news.

"I couldn't wait," Jenny was saying. Not about Davy. About summer. "Now it feels like time has stopped." She faltered. "It's been—" She paused, counting the years since she had had a whole summer off, no classes or tutoring.

"Too long," Tonya said. "Your bathing suit is older than Penny."

Jenny was going to be done with her master's by December. Kev had almost another whole year to go.

"I'm not making any plans," Jenny said. Summer was all she had. How long was that? Then she would keep right on teaching eighth grade social studies, same room, same morning sun, same Thermos and philodendron.

Irene hadn't told Deke that Jenny and Kev were having problems. Jenny had asked her not to, had begged her not to. "Not until it's for sure; maybe it won't be for sure." But when Irene had suggested that maybe their situation was due to stress, Jenny had replied carefully, "There are many people who live as we do and still love each other."

"If it's stress, that can change," Irene had said again. Thinking about Jenny's sweet long summer at home now that she was finishing up her master's, she thought, *Things are already changing.*

Jenny hadn't wanted a big wedding, hadn't even wanted a chapel wedding. "We're going to elope," Jenny had told them. "Only we're telling you."

"Save your money," Kev had added.

Deke had looked at Irene and said, "Well, that works too. Catch ya later," and pulled his hat down and walked on out to the barn, got on his tractor, and drove out across the field, down the swale, leaving the discussion to Irene. It was either that, he told Irene later, or "knock the jerk flat on his ass, and that wouldn't do anything but get the ground dirty." In many ways it had been like that all along with Kev—no captions, just turnings and mostly away, and silence. Irene didn't believe it was possible to squander love, and Jenny was in love. So.

Last Christmas, on a drive home from a mother-daughter shopping trip, Jenny had confided that all was not well in her marriage. When Irene had talked to Jenny about stress and how things were not going to stay the same and that nothing ever did, Jenny, looking hard-eyed and older, had said, "All that's changing is the locks." Then she told Irene how over the past summer Kev had been leaving before seven in the morning to commute to his early class. An eight o'clock again!" Jenny had wailed when he told her. But Jenny had found out there was no eight o'clock class. Kev was simply leaving early, finding a quiet place in the library, and reading magazines and newspapers—newspapers, it turned out, with an eye toward the classifieds. "Mom," Jenny had continued, clearing her throat, "if he takes a job way off—" Here she had swung her hand out, as though pointing across the continent, imagining it all out there, everything she had heard from him in his feverish confession, an arrayed arc of choices: Seattle, Denver, St. Louis, Graceland. Then, sounding very much as she had as a child, she announced, "I'm not going."

Irene had driven five miles before asking, "Will he be back?"

"I'm not leavin' the light on," Jenny had retorted.

Then they had arrived at Jenny's, gotten out of the car, sorted through bags and packages. Irene had taken hen eggs from Mercy and her little bronze and black flock out of the trunk and slipped the basket over Jenny's wrist. Nothing in her lifetime had prepared Jenny for what her mother had to say: "Your daddy will help you with the locks."

They had stood still, just that one more moment, looking at each other, burdened and unburdened.

"You been prayin'?" Irene had looked away. Somebody was coming along the road; they both looked. Silver pickup, king cab. Nobody they knew. They waved anyway.

"Is 'Oh God Oh God Oh God' a prayer?"

"He's heard it before," Irene had said. "Now and then, throw in an Amen."

"You pray too," Jenny had told her, "for that dissertation paper. He's gotta finish by next July." She had turned at the door, glanced back, "Or he'll think it's all been a waste."

All? Irene had wondered.

There were many reasons the flight had been delayed. Sherry and the children and her parents wanted to fly with Davy's casket, and the military plane they could all fly on together was too large to land at Tri-State. Smaller corporate and private jets could hold the passengers but not the casket. The governor himself had been consulted. A solution had been found. Then other difficulties arose in logistics, and then rough weather. By the time the aircraft approached Camden Tri-County, it was coming in through twilight, the sun already below the horizon. Flags were still at half-staff. No one was worried about the governor's sunrise-to-sunset decree at this point. The crowds and the welcomers had not wavered or diminished. This day was far from over.

Davy's family had had a day lived privately, as much as it could be in such a public moment. That isolation—or consideration—had blessed them; they were in a between place, where ticking time had stopped. When the word finally came, Deke nodded, yes, on their way, and Irene—not knowing if any of the others knew about the tattoo, how Sherry had insisted on seeing it if at all possible—stepped close and whispered, "Did she see it?" Deke told her the undertaker had been the one, had borrowed Sherry's phone and taken a picture, close up, nothing else, "Just that, only that," Deke said. "Well," Irene whispered. It was odd how she felt, as though some part of her had hoped. Doubt and hope were alike in some way, and they had gone. They were missed.

Irene stood watching the jet taxi toward them. Deke stood behind her, his right arm around her, his broken hand in a fresh cast pressing against her heart, knowing exactly where she hurt. She could feel his heartbeat against her back. It was one pain between them, connecting them. She laid her right hand on the cast; he had broken his fist punching a hole in the wall when the chaplain and the colonel had come to the door with the news. Now, as their son returned under a U.S. flag, they were wrapped together in a pledge pose. The plane rolled to a stop.

The rest of the journey would be stored in fragments. For days, months, years memories of moments would rise up, swirl, sweep over all of them. Irene would always be gathering them into the one story, twenty-one miles of road from the airport to the churchyard, twenty-nine years long. It was quite dark by the time members of the motorcade left Camden. Escorted, they had no delays and moved at a steady but dignified pace. Cars stopped or moved to the side of the road and parked while they passed. All along the route, past the city limits, there were people waiting, as they had been all day. Candles, flashlights, lanterns: each person offered some light. In the towns there were more people, and their faces were clearer by streetlight, but they were holding candles also. There was at least one person along the road by every mailbox. When the motorcade came to the turn onto Main, the throngs began. A mile down Main they passed Frazier Fabrics, its 24/7 floodlight-lit flag at half-staff. The factory was closed, no night shift. All the workers had been given the afternoon and until noon the next day before they'd have to report for work. On both sides of the street young and old, strangers and friends, neighbors, coworkers, fellow citizens stood in vigil, their faces uplit by the candles.

A mile more and the procession turned at a stoplight. They were almost at the city limits, end of the streetlights and sidewalks. There was Jacky's sign, his truck with headlights on, home-rigged flashers blinking. Jacky, now holding a lantern, had painted GOD BLESS THE WAR. THANK YOU SGT DAVY, along with a heart.

Irene wondered if there had ever before been a funeral at night.

Now the turn at the fire truck and the last three miles to the chapel. The motorcade rolled a little faster past the mailboxes with their flags and yellow ribbons and the candlelit groups standing in the driveways.

An hour was spent in the church, with every possible comfort and hope celebrated. The overflow crowd stood on the porch and steps and continued down into the churchyard and out as far as the road, honoring with silence and attention as they had all day. Whip-poor-wills—the ones crying, "Chuck! Wills! Widow!"—called, heedless of the voices and music from the church. When that part was done, the silvery casket was brought back out again, slow-stepped across the uneven grass and to the grave. The family again took the front seats, and all the rest of the seats except one were filled. Had someone miscounted? Were they all there? Who was missing? It began again with familiar words both true and new, and then came to an end. When this part was done, the folding of the flag began. Those hands—hands of mortal men—worked like machines but driven by passion for honor and perfection so that each tribute of the thirteen folds was perfect, each crease and tuck, tuck, tuck an everlasting triumph over death. The eighth fold had honored the fallen soldier and his mother; the tenth had honored his father. They were all folded into it—everyone there, watching, now folded with Davy into that flag. The flag—its journey from the war zone through this day above the casket, honored glove to glove, perfected, completed—reached the presenter, who slowly turned, knelt before Sherry, and passed the perfect triangle with its field of stars from his hands into hers, on behalf of a grateful nation.

The Guard and the Legion had had all day, and they had figured it out. Vehicles had been parked just so. Headlights washed the dark stripes down the trousers and were reflected in the insignia and brass of the riflemen who fired the three volleys. Fire breathed out from the gun barrels. Davy's baby cried, just a moment, and Sherry turned the child so those great staring eyes could take in everything. The whip-poor-wills hushed. The smoke drifted away.

A one-armed bugler, on the hill in an angle of tiki torches, his shadow wavering into the dark pines, offered "Taps" to the stars. The last note faded away, the final salute ended. As the Honor Guard half-stepped out of their lives, moving down the line of family and then away, the last two who stopped to speak to Irene were the men who had strode through the wheat that evening bringing the news. They had come a long way to this long day. It was almost midnight. Irene didn't know what was next. No one did. People were moving away from the grave and toward the church again so that the workers could seal the vault and backfill. Deke wanted to help despite advice and a broken

86

hand. Irene was walking all around in the crowd, recognizing people, listening, wishing them well.

In the shadows, on the edge of things, a form with windswept angel white hair, unpegged, untamed, and wearing a slim white sundress with a little black jacket that was hardly more than a sketch had caught Irene's eye. It was the oddest thing, how they worked side by side every day and now they were shaking hands.

Kit's hands were shaking. "He was two years ahead of me. I never caught up. You know I had a crush on him forever."

Irene side-stepped on the rough ground and roots. "No." Something dropped inside her so hard she glanced down. Dug in her heels. Made herself look up. Never expecting or knowing what to expect next, but not this. She looked around for Deke. Where was Deke?

"Kid stuff," Kit said. "He didn't know me. Never even noticed me." Her voice broke. Kit stamped her right foot, like a doe about to bolt, wobbled on those tall shoes. Irene put out a hand to steady her.

For the life of her Irene couldn't think of a kind thing to say but the truth. "I bet he noticed."

"Nope," Kit explained. "You never heard of me before that first day at work." Irene waited. "You would've. Yes?"

Irene considered.

Kit added, "He didn't even recognize me that day at the plant. Nah." She slowly drew in a deep breath and more slowly exhaled. A silence ensued. Two trucks and a car drove off into the night. A brief spatter of laughter came from across the churchyard, and heads turned. So did theirs. Suddenly Kit awkwardly embraced and released Irene back into the moil and flow. "He's the best, that's all. But you already know that." She turned, to move on.

"There's—" Irene began.

"Why I keep lookin'."

In the church Vicki Malachy gave up the search for the lighter, and with the last cigarette from the pack between her black lips she headed up the aisle to the candle flames on the altar. Vicki had gone pierced and

Goth over the summer. Everything about her bore the glint and scorch of hell. Ask around; ask her mother, who'd done everything but put a warning in the personals in the paper: to whom it may concern, as of this date I am no longer responsible for debts public and private and so on and on and on. Vicki had a new way to push her mother's buttons. "Say something!" Juki would yell. Vicki would reply, "Dot dot dot," with smoke rings.

She leaned flat-palmed on the open Bible, her body already beginning to show the new anonymous pregnancy. She had on what she thought of as her lucky black leather miniskirt, black ankle boots, and a studded black vest over a sleeveless tee. When she couldn't get the skirt zipped anymore, she had bored a hole to either side of the placket and installed a chain and padlock. A brilliant solution as she saw it, for she could adjust it out, link by link, for as long as she could drag the skirt over her belly. Oh and she would. Some instinct caused her to turn, her jaw still jutted from lighting the cigarette, to look toward the back of the church. Juki was there, silent as a mouse. She had slipped in and seated herself by the baby carrier, beaming out disappointment.

"I never was exactly the Bride o' Christ," Vicki exhaled around the cigarette. "Get over it." Last month's purple highlights in her spiky dark hair were now red. She felt one of the pages, stuck to her palm by sweat, tear or give along the spine. She turned back to it, pushed the wide satin bookmark aside, gathered a chunk of pages, and heaved them over deeper into the good news. She put the bookmark back, but the torn-away page showed, so she opened to it and then folded it over itself. This time nothing showed. Except Vicki's rounding belly. After last summer's scare, after a lull, Vicki had found another lone wolf in the dark.

"Say something I want to hear," Vicki dared.

"You took the words right out of my mouth," Juki returned. She would have said more, but one of the church ladies came in, stepped behind the pulpit, and rummaged around on the shelf. "I've got one!" she called to someone in the kitchen. They were about to light the chafing dishes. She glanced at Vicki, at Juki. Old story. "Don't mind me," she said, and trotted out holding a lighter in her fist. They weren't making much noise back there, no chatter, just the necessary sounds of work: directions, last-minute rearrangements, chair scrapes, and adjustments.

Vicki headed back toward her mother after checking behind the pulpit also, in case there was another lighter. She'd have been glad to have it, one less thing to buy.

Juki was holding up the baby's bottle, sniffing it. The baby had been asleep, was still asleep. Juki thought she knew now what had cured its colic.

"No, it's not apple juice," Vicki said before her mother could.

Now Juki was leaned over, sniffing the baby.

"Beer?" she asked. "You mixed beer with the juice?"

Vicki blessed her with a radiant smile. "Why waste the juice?"

From the hall doorway, one of the kitchen crew beckoned, "Ladies? Come in for the blessing."

Juki stood. She had brought food, enough for her family and more. She moved forward, taking the baby carrier and, after a moment's thought, the bottle bag and the rest of the kit with her. As she eased past, Vicki took the bottle, tipped it up, finished it off, and slid it into the mesh pocket on the tote. They were both relieved when Vicki, with plans already made, exited the side door and landed with a clump to the ground rather than face the people coming up the steps headed in to supper.

Irene and Deke and their family were at the front tables being waited on. The rest of the people would serve themselves, buffet style, from the lined and laden tables. Juki set the baby and the kit beside her chair. She detoured toward Irene to lean down and speak a moment. Her one hand gripped the edge of the paper tablecloth while the other balanced the food she'd brought, and she whispered, "It wasn't supposed to be like this," before moving on.

Irene wouldn't leave until the grave was filled and smoothed, the flowers carpeted it, and the fake green turf carpet and folding chairs were loaded into the van—going, going, gone. Even then she and Deke remained. Family and friends had children to care for, stock to see to even at that hour, and work the next day. This tremendous and staggering time-out between before and after was almost over. When the church ladies had finished clearing things inside, they wrung and hung the towels on the wooden rack, then made sure lights were off and windows and doors locked. The lot and field emptied. Irene and Deke walked out one more time across the trampled grass to the undertaker's canopy, the only shelter from all those stars, to thank the men who had used shovels, no backhoe, to fill the grave by hand. It didn't matter how many times she said it; she would offer it to each and all. It was no trouble; it was for Davy. "Thank you" was her theme, and her mantra—the mother's prayer—was "Safe home."

When they arrived home, the dusk-to-dawns were on out at the chicken houses and by the barn. They were automatic. The surprise was the porch light. "Oh," Irene said, heartsick. "I wonder where Mercy is." She had not thought of her little free-range Sebright once all day. While Deke headed to the barn, Irene turned and surveyed the lot, the fence lines, the fields. No frog song now, and she could almost count the cricket sounds between the lulls. The pond looked black and was so still the stars twinkled in it.

Deke returned with the news, "Somebody did up the chores." He had his gloves with him, had forgotten to put them on the shelf. He tapped his leg with them up the grassy slope to the house. There was going to be dew, and neither one of them had on farm shoes. The stepping-stones were single-file. Deke let Irene have them and walked by her side, vigilant. Even after the short nights and long day, he was on patrol. He had learned the hard way what he would never forget: there was something out there, always something out there. For a moment he stopped, turned, and looked back, doing a slow reconnaissance of the dark lines and corners. Irene paused beside him. She was used to it. They didn't speak, but when he shook his head, she moved on in step with him.

90

As they came around the thicket of hydrangeas taller than Irene, they could see the porch. They had company. Sua Nag was asleep in a chair, tucked into herself tidy and small, and K'shaundra had fallen back and settled atilt in the swing with one long leg on the floor. Both waked instantly and fully when Irene exclaimed, "Mercy!" There she was in her little crate on the wall. The light glinted from her eye, but she didn't fly down.

It was harder on Deke because he couldn't think of anything at all to say. And he couldn't leave. And he wouldn't cry. Irene knew what to do: open up; let everyone in; listen. For a little while it was all K'shaundra, not hiding her battered face now that they'd seen it. Link had busted away from custody, the best she could explain it, shoving guards, stealing a gun, and then stealing the transport van, shooting, wrecking, and taking to the woods. He had found her. But this time she had a cell phone and managed to connect before he broke in. He was out of bullets, so he beat her with the stolen gun. That's why she'd missed work, missed hearing the news about Davy, and why she'd stayed away from the church. Link was gone. He'd already been taken away. There'd be no trial; he'd messed all that up this time and was in a federal prison somewhere. She'd waited till dark to walk over from the farmhouse and started the chores first, so if there was someone at the house, church ladies or friends doing things around, she could slip back home without being seen at all. "Then I recalled that little chicken needed her step-up stick," she told them.

Then it was Sua Nag's turn. She drew the story in the air with her hands, acting it out, and when it got to the good part, everybody went out on the porch and K'shaundra and Sua Nag performed the ballet together. Sua Nag imitated Mercy, stepping in place on the porch floor to show how the hen had fidgeted on the railing, looking up at the crate on the wall with her left eye, then her right eye, then her left eye again. They had figured out about the little ladder Deke had made and had been about to put it in place. Mercy had seen it and hopped down from the railing, ready to climb, when—

"Boom!" K'shaundra hollered. "Boom!" And then together, "Boom!"

Irene and Deke jumped and grabbed hold of each other. Mercy eased up into a crouch in her crate, craning down. K'shaundra and Sua Nag were trying to convey their shock, surprise, and terror when noise from the concerted gunfire volleys during the funeral salute had rolled across the valley and crashed into the farm buildings and their ears. Sua Nag had from long and old instinct dropped to the floor on one side of the hen, and K'shaundra had done the same on the other side. Instinct in each had said, "It's back" or "He's back," and both had dived to cover the most vulnerable of all, but they had missed. Before they could save her, Mercy had flown straight up—never mind the ladder—a sudden rattling whuff of a launch across the porch, right up into her crate on the wall. Then she had shaken herself, turned, and curtsied into place. K'shaundra and Sua Nag ended the story right there, with a similar curtsy. Everybody laughed.

"Then we waited to see if the light bothered her awake, but she stayed put," K'shaundra explained.

"We stay put," Sua Nag added with that way she had of not looking.

There was a pause then, and Irene asked them to come back inside so Mercy could get her beauty sleep. But they gave quick good-byes and didn't linger. Just like that, then, K'shaundra vanished around the side of the house, and Sua Nag found her way to her little car, turned it around, probed her way out to the county road, and was gone.

Deke and Irene moved quietly through their house turning lights on, turning lights off, finding comfort. Later in bed they lay side by side, his right foot and her left foot touching. Nothing had changed that mustn't. It was still night, still dark, but the dark wasn't empty. It teemed with dreamers and vigils. When daylight came, there would be something to do with love.

"She had thought she was done with sewing, with being dragged forward all day with the cloth as it goes under the needle, doing her part, but never finishing anything, just shoving her piece on and picking up the next one. Now she was thanking God for the second chance."

"Like all the great writers, Mary Hood has mastered the high wires of brevity and conciseness. Her deeply imagined characters ... speak as if they are offering their own true and often fabulous commentary on the book of life itself."

PAT CONROY, author of *The Death of Santini*

"Mary Hood puts her fine gifts of scene-setting and characterization to work in this compact saga of a rural sewing factory and the women bound by hard times to its ever-running machinery. Hood highlights the plentiful humor of her cast, and, in the face of a community tragedy, a humanity and warmth beyond all expectations."

DOT JACKSON, author of *Refuge*

MARY HOOD is the author of the novel *Familiar Heat* and two short story collections, *How Far She Went* (winner of the Flannery O'Connor Award for Short Fiction and the *Southern Review*/LSU Short Fiction Award) and *And Venus Is Blue* (winner of the Lillian Smith Award, the Townsend Prize for Fiction, and the Dixie Council of Authors and Journalists Author of the Year Award). Hood has won the Whiting Writers' Award, the Robert Penn Warren Award, and a Pushcart Prize and was a 2014 inductee into the Georgia Writers Hall of Fame.

STORY RIVER BOOKS

Pat Conroy, editor at large

Seam Busters explores the connections we make to one another, from the simplest acts to those moments that define life and death. When Irene Morgan returns to Frazier Fabrics, a family-owned cotton mill in Ready, Georgia, she joins an eclectic group of women workers sharing their interwoven lives inside and outside the factory. Under constant surveillance and beholden to production quotas and endless protocols presented under the auspices of "American Pride," the women sew state-of-the-art camouflage for U.S. troops fighting in Afghanistan, one of whom is Irene's son.

As Irene toils under the stress of the learning curve and production goals, she comes to embrace the camaraderie of her peers, some of whom play on the mill's bowling team, the Seam Busters. She comes to know Coquita, a shaky veteran returned from three tours in the Middle East; Kit, an angel-haired rule breaker unlucky in love; the stoic Hmong woman Sue Nag; the beaten but not yet defeated K'shaundra; and Jacky, a well-intentioned fool determined to be heard. In time Irene comes to value bonds with this motley crew.

ISBN 978-1-61117-498-4 $15.95

9 781611 174984

Photograph by Keith Mc

THE UNIVERSITY OF SOUTH CAROLINA PRESS
COLUMBIA, SOUTH CAROLINA 29

www.sc.edu/uscp